I0553386

MICHAEL
A HOLY GHOST STORY

C.Y. DAVENPORT

MICHAEL
A HOLY GHOST STORY
BY: C.Y. DAVENPORT

Copyright 2021 @ C.Y. DAVENPORT

Originally self-published in 2021. This edition published in 2025.

ISBN-13: 979-8-218-63745-3

Manufactured in the United States of America

Since I was a little girl ALL I have ever wanted was 2 little boys. To Xavier and Christian, I truly thank God for the beautiful young men you have become, you are brilliant, kind, strong and more importantly, you know Jesus Christ as your Lord and Savior. I am so Godly proud of the young men you have become. Thank you for all of your support in life and completing this book. Next to Mom (your Granny), you have been my greatest cheerleaders.

Chapter 1

"In a time of intense darkness, a ray of hope comes through a child."

This is my all-time favorite quote from my favorite author, J Elliott. I have always quoted this rather haphazardly, but it was never truer than in this story.

My name is Xavier Christian. I dropped my last name when I began my professional career. I am 24 years old, and I am a neophyte reporter for the *Washington Post*.

It seems my whole life I have been searching for my purpose. I had always known it would come through writing.

I have been with the *Post* exactly one year, to the day that I was sent on the most fascinating story.

I was assigned to go into Zimbabwe, Africa, to meet the oldest living man in the world. The most successful neophyte reporter did this every June. It was a foundational cultural story for the paper, since its inception. Also, it was designed to give the neophyte reporter a well-earned rest in an exotic place.

This year, it was my turn.

I was going to see a man who was documented as being 115 years old, but it was believed he was even older than that.

Normally, this would be a one to two-day assignment. One would speak with a relative about the highlight of the subject's life, what a day for a person of this age consists of, take a few pictures of the person and their home, enjoy a mini vacation in an exotic place, and then return. But absolutely nothing could have prepared me for the story of which I heard.

This is that documented account.

I arrived at 9:45 a.m., African time.

I had been traveling for more than 23 hours, and was totally exhausted when I deplaned and saw my name on a large poster.

I walked over, and said, "Yes I am Xavier Christian."

The driver was sent from our sister local newspaper, the *Zimbabwe Gazette*. He introduced himself as Zahede.

Zahede simply said, "I am a reporter, as well, but I am here to take you to your hotel, and through the city and country, while you work on your story."

He was about 45 years old, tall and thin, and he spoke excellent English.

He took my bag and put it in a small jeep, which had *Zimbabwe Gazette* on it.

He then took me to the African hotel, called the Trampezie.

I asked Zahede if I had an interpreter. He smiled and said, "You will not need one. I will be back to pick you up at 11:30 am for your 1:00 pm appointment."

I went to my room and unpacked, showered, ate, and prepared for my afternoon trip into the jungle to meet Mr. Michael Finn. The oldest living man in the world.

I was called by Zahede at exactly 11:30 am.

I gathered all of my equipment. A still camera, a video camcorder, a tape recorder, a satchel full of writing utensils, and my laptop. The most fascinating journey of my life would soon begin.

As we traveled in the small *Gazette* jeep and left the confines of the city, I noticed how beautiful Africa really was. Everything looked so lush and green in the summer. Much more so here than in America. It is as if the jungle was alive. The flowers were vibrant. The colors were magnificently orange, purple, pink, and yellow.

The sounds in the jungle were rich, and the colors of the animals were so crisp, that you almost wanted to touch them. I fought the urge because the animals were wild. I saw elephants, gazelles, lions, birds of all types, and just about every exotic animal you could think of. I took pictures of all of it.

I had originally thought my driver, Zahede, who spoke perfect English, would be my interpreter. As we continued, Zahede said I would love Mr. Mike, as he was affectionately called around here.

I said, "I am sure," all the time thinking to myself he will probably sleep through the entire interview.

As we continued, Zahede said, "I hope you can keep up."

It was at this point that I became a little baffled.

Keep up with a 115-year-old man?

How difficult could that be?

You see, honestly, I expected this person to be too old to move, let alone communicate.

As we continued, we came to a quaint house.

It was amazing. Like something right out of a Rockwell painting, including a white picket fence.

I had expected to go to a small dirt hut. What I arrived at was a medium-sized brown brick home, with a porch and a chimney.

When I opened the fence and walked through, I saw beautiful vibrant flowers and fruit trees. Then I saw the most amazing display of colors I had ever seen. There were at least 100 multi-colored butterflies. They were pastel blue, yellow, green, and pink, and swarming all around the flowers.

There were lines of multi-colored roses that lined the concrete sidewalk.

I had expected nothing like this.

As we walked up the stairs to the home, I saw two rockers on a dark wood porch that was so clean it almost looked shellacked. I was going to knock on the door when I saw a beautiful doorbell. It had writing around it, "As for me and my house we will serve the Lord."

When I pushed the doorbell, it played the most beautiful melody I had ever heard. I recalled that melody some years ago, but had not heard it since I was a child.

The peace in this environment was so tangible, you could almost cut it with a knife. An older woman, maybe in her 40s, answered the door. She was small with a beautiful bronzish black skin color. She had long, curly black hair. She knew my name, but I was at a loss for hers.

I said, "You must be his great, great, great, granddaughter."

She smiled very sweetly, and said, "I am his daughter. My name is Ms. Dottie but thank you."

"But you can't be over 50 years old," I exclaimed. She thanked me again and simply smiled.

Zahede helped me bring my things and said he would pick me up at 8:00 p.m.

He hugged Ms. Dottie and they exchanged greetings. She asked how his family was doing and he said that they were doing fine, and that he would bring his boys this weekend for more of Mr. Mike's stories. His boys, I found out, were 9 and 11, and they loved to hear Mr. Mike tell stories of his adventures.

"Tell them I will make them their favorite dessert again."

"They will love that," Zahede replied. He had to go and told me he would see me later.

I looked around, and noticed how immaculate the home was kept. There were hardwood floors that were polished to a shine.

The home was beautifully furnished. It was full of windows, so the house was well lit. The smell of fresh cut flowers filled the house.

We went past a beautiful dining set on our way to Mr. Mike's study.

The dining room had a beautiful cherry wood curio cabinet, a China cabinet, and a huge octagon dining table with high back wood carved chairs.

I stumbled past it, on our way to the study.

The study was made of rich dark wood full of books from the floor to the ceiling.

Ms. Dottie said; "Father, this is Xavier Christian. The reporter from the *Washington Post*."

The large dark brown leather chair swirled around, and I could not believe my eyes.

How could this be a 115-year-old man?

He popped out of the chair and stood to his feet. He stood 6'4", about 230 pounds, and his hair was barely grey. He had a strong face and his whole body seemed muscular.

Again, how could this be a 115-year-old man?

There must be some mistake.

He shook my hand with great vigor, pulled me to him, and gave me a great big bear hug.

He then pushed me back, and smiled.

"Yes," he said, observing me. "Yes. I can see the resemblance."

His English was perfect.

I said, "Pardon me, sir. Have we met?"

Without answering me, he said, "Have a seat."

Shocked, I said, "Mr. Mike how can this be? You barely look 50 years of age. Does this phenomenon run in your family"?

He simply smiled and said, "I have good genes, and I remain healthy because I have a very important matter to accomplish before I leave this earth. I need a strong and healthy body to complete it. Do you have a bible?

"Yes," I replied.

"Then you must have read where it says 'Righteousness is a beautifier.'"

"I don't recall that scripture."

"Well, it's there, and, as you can see, it's also very true."

He showed me to a comfortable leather brown chair in the room, and sat across from me in an identical chair.

"Now, young man. What can I do for you?"

As I sat there, my mouth still open by his appearance, I looked at my notes.

"Please tell me about your childhood," I stammered, rather poorly. I had expected to speak with a relative of his. Not the man, himself. I found myself rearranging my questions somewhat.

He sat up, looked out of the window the chairs were positioned at, and gazed for a moment.

Then he said, "Ever since I was a very small boy, I could see things that other people seemed to not notice. I never knew my mother, and my relationship with my father was strained at best.

"The dark things that I saw every day of my life were really the only companions I had.

"I was born in Perfect California."

"So was I," I replied, "my whole family still lives there."

He simply smiled, "I know." Without missing a beat, he then continued his story, "There are no records of my birth, because of what I was birthed for. I was to be a 6th generation warlock, a regional warlock."

"What is that?"

"It simply means I was responsible for a region of the world to do my masters bidding. My father, the current regional warlock's territory encompassed all of North America, in addition to Canada and Mexico.

"Our job was to spread darkness throughout the world. If we could do this successfully, we would be made rich beyond our dreams on earth, and would be given a place in Hell to rule with the father of darkness.

"I had been dedicated to the dark one every three years of my life. When I first turned three, I was dedicated in Morocco. Then in Europe, at age six. And then in Sweden, at age nine. At each dedication, I received a new voice that would lead and direct me. Then, at age 12, I was to be dedicated in Africa. Zimbabwe to be exact."

"The day we arrived in Africa was to be my final dedication. I was extremely excited to see all of my old friends, if you could call them that, I only saw them every three years. They were the only children I was ever allowed to associate with.

"We came together for our final dedication, where I would receive the position of 20th region warlock. When we arrived, we were well received, as always.

"I was introduced as the next chancellor of the 20th region elect to several dignitaries, important businessmen, and world leaders.

"On our way to the room, I noticed a young girl, about my age, standing in the hotel lobby, as if she was waiting for someone. She had this absolutely magnificent light that appeared to come from her. Since my father was talking, I began to walk over to her. My voices immediately objected.

"Normally I never disobeyed them. I was taught that they were my guides, and that they were there to help and protect me. But I was almost drawn to this young girl. The voices were now shouting at me, telling me to stay away from her, but I had to know what this light was.

"I could somehow sense the absolute purity of its power, and I had to know what she was. I had seen plenty of white witches that had white light, but nothing compared to this. This light was brilliant, and magnificently marvelous. There were no words to describe it. The closer I got, the fainter my voices became. It was as if I had left them behind.

"I asked her, 'What are you?'

"'What am I?' She asked.

"'The Light,' I said. I could almost feel its warmth. I could actually feel the thing I had longed for my whole life.

"Love. Even though I never knew what that could possibly feel like, I knew that was what it was.

"'Are you a white witch?'

"She stood straight, gave me her hand, and said, 'My name is Nina Finn, and I am a Christian.'

"I have seen Christians before, but none of them had this type of power. It was much more powerful than anything I or my father had, and my father was a chancellor. My father had many Christians in our home, but none of them had this type of power. I always thought they were powerless against us.

"I then introduced myself. 'My name is Tykellie. It means 'dark warrior' in Latin. I am the 6th generation regional warlock elect.' The latter I said with great pride.

"She simply said, 'Oh, we are praying for you, and now we have a name.

"'Pray for me?' I asked. 'We are wealthy beyond your understanding. Our father has done that for us, which is why we serve him, and one day, we will rule with him.'

"She seemed to ignore the whole statement, and said, 'We are having a meeting tomorrow morning at 9:00 am, right here in this hotel in the dining hall.' She pointed to the hall 'Would you like to come?'

"I said I was forbidden to attend such things. I wondered if father knew that Christians had real power, and thought maybe we were on the wrong side.

"The thoughts in my mind began to run rampant.

"Just then Nina's father called her, and she said, 'I have to go, but we will be praying for you. Remember, 9:00 am tomorrow morning. try to make it.'

"I just stood there, trying to figure out what had happened to me.

"Then my voices came back, with a vengeance. They cursed at me. Told me she was a liar. They put so much pressure on me, that I was on the floor, struggling to breathe.

"Just then, father came to me, picked me up, and asked, 'What have you done?'

"I said, 'Nothing. I saw a real Christian. Did you know they have power?'

"My father, who typically never showed emotions, was noticeably upset. I could not believe that he was doing so. It was as if he had no control. Father was always in control.

"'How would you know that? Did you see one? Did you talk to one? Stay away from them!'

"He practically dragged me through the lobby of the hotel.

"'Did I not tell you, where the real power lies!'

"Even though I never felt a connection with my father, I always obeyed him without question.

"The hotel was beautiful. It was trimmed in gold with crystal chandeliers. I remember thinking how beautiful it appeared, as I was being dragged through it. I dared not bring up the topic with him again. I just went to my room and changed.

"I was starving, but was not allowed to eat before the final dedication.

"I was a little nervous. I was about to meet the chief of all regional warlocks, Ubakuta himself. The one who controlled the whole world by controlling the regional warlocks. What an honor. I hoped I would measure up.

"After we were prepared, we went back down the elevators to the lobby. I saw Nina again.

"I wanted to speak to her, but dared not.

"I told my father, 'Look see that fire, see that light?'

"He almost hissed as he tugged my arm and pulled me out the door.

"We got into a jeep. As we left the confines of the city, I noticed how beautiful it was there. I found there was a lot of wealth in Africa, if you knew where to look. We went to what appeared to be a mansion right in the middle of nowhere. It was white, with a huge black rod iron fence surrounding it.

"There were huge trees and beautiful flowers everywhere. I saw all types of animals roaming, but none on the property. I thought that was odd, but understood when I got out of the jeep, as the land felt foreboding.

"We walked up to what looked like about a 100-foot-high door. The butler opened it, just as we walked up to it. He showed us through the house. I felt strange as I walked through the long hall to our destination. I stayed close to my father as we came to a room where all of the warlocks and their sons were already sitting around a huge marble table.

"Everyone turned when we came into the room. All the boys slightly smiled at me as we came in the room. We were all so deprived of friends, we looked forward to seeing each other.

"In the front of the room was a huge black marble altar, as usual, but this time there were three goats tied to it. We were the last to take our seats. I saw three huge goblets. One was silver, one was gold, and one was jeweled encrusted."

It was at that time that Ms. Dottie said, "It's time for dinner."

Where did the time go? it was already 6:00 pm.

"Would you like to stay for dinner?"

"Yes," I said.

Ms. Dottie prepared baked chicken with green beans, beats, hot wheat cornbread, and sweet iced tea.

It was a wonderful meal.

Ms. Dottie said, "You are welcome to stay for dinner but please no history while we are at the table."

She said she had heard the stories a thousand times. I reluctantly agreed and Mr. Mike began to ask me about my life.

"Well," I said "I was born in Perfect, California, as you know. It is probably the most peaceful place in America right now. The public schools are really Christian schools. It is a small town and everyone is genuinely concerned about everyone.

"I left because my whole life, all I ever wanted to do was be a reporter. I graduated from the local college and got a paid internship at a newspaper in New York City, and after two years I got my first big break.

"I am now at the Washington Post and have been there for a full year now. I found the real world to be much less perfect than Perfect, California.

"I come from a long line of preachers, and was always told that God had a plan for my life. I believed them, but never had the desire to be a preacher, like my 4 brothers. I always wanted to write. My mother said I was making up stories and taking pictures from the womb."

"Your family sounds wonderful," Mr. Mike said.

"Thank you," I said, "but I wanted adventure. I wanted to be on the cutting edge of what was going on in the world. I frankly thought being a preacher didn't really fit into who I was. However, my relatives could tell stories that could almost persuade the most devoted journalist to preach.

"I remembered all of the stories my father and grandfather would tell. Instead of living them, I just wanted to write about them. I thought that was just what they were meant to be, but I always wanted to write."

Mrs. Dottie asked after we completed our meal, "Would you like to have your coffee in the sunroom?"

Mr. Mike said, "Yes thank you."

We walked through the home and I saw a wonderful picture of Mr. Mike.

"How old were you there?"

"About 50," he said.

"You don't look a day over that now. How do you do it?"

"Keep listening and I will get to that."

We sat down in the small room. I saw the most beautiful sunset I had ever seen.

I told him that, "Most sunrooms face the east so people can enjoy the sunrise, but yours is on the west side. I guess so you can enjoy the sunset. Right?"

He smiled and said, "Very observant."

Mrs. Dottie brought our coffee and two very large pieces of chocolate cake. My favorite.

"Please continue Mr. Mike."

"Okay," he said. "Where were we? Oh yes.

"I sat down with my father. Then Ubakuta seemed to appear out of thin air. He stood about 6'7, 250 pounds. He appeared to be very strong and muscular. His voice was very heavy and his speech very clear. The foreboding became much stronger but I noticed that my voices were extremely content with him.

"He addressed the group and explained, 'We are in a warfare and we must win. This is your final dedication and you will be given all the power your fathers have. You will be molded into masters of the art of darkness.'

"At that time, all stood, including myself, and put the cloaks that were on the back of the chairs on. After we placed our hoods on, the first regional warlock went to the front. At the stroke of midnight,

Ubakuta cut his hand and put the blood in the gold chalice. Every regional warlock and father then followed suit. Then us regional warlock elects were asked to extend our hands to be cut as we walked one by one past the altar. Ubakuta sliced our hands and put the blood into the silver chalice. After we all sat down, Ubakuta took the three goats and slit their throats. Their blood poured into the multi-jeweled chalice.

"The dedication began at that point. The air became musty, as usual, but this time I could physically see the spirits standing. There was 20 of them. The blood of the elects was poured on the altar until it ran over the sides.

"At that time the first elect warlock was called. He was given the gold chalice to drink from, and then the jeweled chalice. Ubakuta laid hands on him and the darkness entered him. This time I could see a physical change take place. The boy became cold and hard, and looked almost unfeeling. I had never seen this take place before. This went on for each elect, until it was my turn.

"I drank the blood, but when Ubakuta laid hands on me the last spirit of darkness did not enter into me. Ubakuta tried again, but the thing did not or could not enter into me. I was prepared, but something appeared to be hindering it. I could not figure out the problem but I could hear Nina saying, 'I will be praying for you.'

"Father stood up, puzzled and angry at the same time. All 20 of the master warlocks were called to assist Ubakuta and, for what seemed like an eternity, they all tried to help the spirit take possession of me, but the darkness never came to me. It stood there, as if being held back.

"The children were dismissed to a great hall, and I was told to go with them. I walked outside, hoping to get a chance to play.

"My best friends were Junofin from Switzerland and Spamilly from Morocco.

"When I went outside, all of the children seemed aloof and very standoffish. At every other dedication we all played together. The jokes were rather crude, but I had won at the last dedication because I had placed a spell on my teacher who was a witch, and caused her to convulse so much that she actually threw up her liver. I had it documented on video so I had the honor for three years.

"Looking back, you would have thought that I would have known there was something very wrong with the way I was living. My father congratulated me, and when the teacher died, he simply got me another. I had done well in his eyes. Life meant nothing to him.

"Who was the most powerful and who could cause the most destruction were the guidelines for the game, and basically anything went.

"At our 2nd dedication, Spamilly had won by turning his instructor into a dog. He did not look like a dog, but for one week he ate dog food, licked himself, and lived outside. Spamilly had this documented, as well. He had caused that man to lose his mind.

"We were all looking forward to our final dedication. To see who would hold this honor into adulthood. I had finally mastered levitation, and had levitated our dog over the pool and dropped him in.

"I was excited about this. It was not as destructive, but levitation was reserved for senior warlocks, and I had mastered it early. But no one seemed to care. They all stared at me so sternly. I went back down the hall to go to the bathroom.

"While I was trying to find it, I went past Ubukatu's office and I heard him say, 'Has a real Christian prayed for him?'

"'No,' father explained. 'Everything in his life has been controlled. All of his instructors were hand-picked. No unsupervised TV, radio, internet. Nothing. No one. How can this be? 12 years down the drain.'

"As I heard this I remembered what Nina said.

"'We will be praying for you.'

"Ubukatu said, 'You know what must be done.'

"A cold chill ran down my back when he said this. I did not know what would take place, but I knew it would not be good.

"I slipped out of the hall, to the outdoors. I mustered up the energy and asked, 'Who wants to play?'

"Spamilly looked at me, and said, 'Don't you understand? You were not accepted.'

"They gathered around and began to beat me unmercifully. I cried out for father to help me. The beating seemed to go on for an eternity, before father reached in and grabbed me. Not with compassion, but out of disgust. He dragged me to the jeep without a word.

"We went back to the hotel. I got out of the jeep, very disheveled, and walked straight to the elevator.

"When we got back to the room, my father said, 'Purify yourself.'

"I went into my room, stripped down to my underwear, and began to chant.

"Father drew a large pentagram in the middle of my bedroom floor as I changed. He then led me to the center, and began to chant with me.

"When it started it was about three in the morning. When I opened my eyes again it was 7:00 a.m., and I was starving. For some reason, the purification did not have the effect it normally had on me. My voices were not kind to me, but insulting, cursing, and pressuring my body so much so that I felt totally rejected.

"I was so hungry I could hardly think, but I dared not say anything to my father while he was in mediation. I could see him across the living room in his bedroom.

"Then I noticed a door open, and a cart with a large tray of food come into the room. Father did not move, so I jumped up and ate my fill. Then I went back to my room and sat in the pentagram. It was later, I found that room services were ordered from the room next door, but was accidentally brought to our room.

"I began to meditate, again, rather haphazardly, when I heard the door open again. Someone stepped in and removed the cart. I sat back in the pentagram, and instead of mediating, I went to sleep.

"I could see Nina in my dreams saying, 'We will be praying for you,' but every time I would see her, my voices would torment me viciously and darkness would overtake her. Again and again, that is what I dreamt until I awoke at 8:45 a.m.

"I remembered as soon as I opened my eyes that Nina said there would be a meeting in the dining hall of the hotel, at 9:00 a.m.

"I knew I did not have long. Father slept very little and was always through mediating by 10 every morning. I got up, got dressed, and attempted to leave the room, but then suddenly, I was struck down.

"However, I could see Nina say, 'We will be praying for you,' and the pressure would leave.

"There was an intense battle as I struggled to get to the elevator. I was forced to the floor again. I could see Nina say, 'We are praying for you,' and I was able to rise and continue.

"By the time I got to the hotel lobby, I moved very slowly, because my limbs felt like they were being held. The closer I got to the dining hall, the more my mobility seemed to return. As I continued to walk, all of the pressure and attacks subsided.

"I saw Nina and her father at the head table. I slid behind the curtain in the back of the room, just in time to hear them say, 'There is a battle going on, but we would win.'

"Ubukatu's words exactly.

"I thought: Were we fighting each other? Light against darkness. Was I on the wrong side?

"Here I felt love and acceptance. Light. Peace. it was wonderful. Then I looked at Nina's father, standing at the podium. You should have seen it. He was flanked by two massive angels. They were about 10 feet tall, with drawn golden swords. Their faces shown like lightning. They had golden breastplates on. Their wing span was about 11 feet high and 8 feet across. They had massive cannonball muscles in their arms. They were magnificent in every sense of the word.

"I had never seen such a display of power. Father would have had large, powerful, dark looking shadowy creatures with blood-red eyes. Their armor was silver along with their swords. I use to think that was power, but I must have been deceived, for by comparison, there was none. I also noticed father was only flanked by these creatures when he was entertaining so-called Christians.

"Now, for the first time in my life, I began to question where the power really was. It was obvious the darkness would not come near the light. What was wrong?

"'Jesus,' he spoke the name so reverently. What a beautiful name. I had only heard it used in swear words so I assumed that that was what it was. Nina's father continued, 'Only by accepting Him as savior can you have power over the darkness. Saying you are sorry for your sins and accepting His sacrifice is the only way to God. we must convey this wholeheartedly to mankind.'

"He almost appeared to be looking at me, and his words pierced my heart.

"'God has a better plan. Movies, radio, TV, magazines. All of these avenues are constantly glorifying darkness, which can cost mankind their eternal souls. It is our job in the earth to not allow this to happen.'

"I looked at the clock on the wall, and knew I had to hurry back to my room before Father came out of his meditation. As I drew closer to the elevator, my voices came back, and the pressure was so intense that, by the time I got to the elevator, I was on the floor writhing in pain. I crawled to my room and into my bed. It was then I remembered the name: JESUS.

"I recited the prayer I heard Nina's father say. I called on him, and it stopped. The pressure. The pain. The screaming. Everything stopped.

"I felt clean. Pure. Light as a feather.

"I took off my clothes and crawled back into the pentagram before father noticed I was gone.

"He came in, and said, 'Get dressed.'

"I did, and thought surely he'd notice something, but he did not.

"This JESUS was more powerful than my father.

"We headed out to Ubukatu's home. I remembered the way we went in. I was again forced to strip down and get inside the pentagram. This pentagram was inside a blood-red room with an upside-down cross. I was told to recite the dedication, and that is what I did for the remainder of the day until 11 at night.

"At that time, all of the senior and junior warlocks came in, dressed in their black hooded robes. I was given a robe and sandals, and led outside to an open black altar that was attached to a portable furnace. I started to run, but was grabbed and held down by the senior warlocks, including my father.

"'Father! Help me! Help me!'

"I was strapped down and bound hand and feet. They had tied me down to the altar and slid me into the portable furnace. I jumped and squirmed on the grill. I could not get out. Then I heard the sound of fire.

"WOOOSH!!!

"I knew it was too late, but I remembered the name JESUS. I called him.

"He could save me, I thought.

"Just then, I was covered in the most marvelous light, and two huge angels with huge wings were on each side of me.

"They said nothing, but enclosed me in their wings."

Chapter 2

"I must have passed out. All I remembered then was waking up. The furnace had holes in it, so I could see the sunlight.

"It was then I realized I was no longer bound to the furnace. My hands and feet were free. I pushed open the door and went outside.

"Since my bands were burned off around my feet and hands, I could easily move out onto the altar. I saw my clothes folded up on the ground, along with my shoes. I had no idea how they had gotten there, because I remembered I had not worn them outside.

"I dressed quickly and could see Ubukatu's home over the huge trees. I knew to go in the opposite direction but, where would I go?

"I simply began to wonder through the forest, not knowing which direction I was gong.

"As I continued to walk I could tell I was coming to a clearing. It was then I saw Nina's father standing there.

"'Mr. Finn.'

"'Michael' he called to me. 'You will live with me now.'

"I was still dazed, so Mr. Finn took me by the arm and helped me to his car. I was extremely week after the ordeal. It was only by the grace of God that I made it out of the dense woods alive. I found out later that it was about a mile walk, but…" Mr. Mike said with great fervor, "There is a GOD!!!."

He continued, "Mr. Finn took me to his home and got me cleaned up and fed. I slept for about 17 hours after that. It was about seven the next morning when I woke up in this very different, but loving home. The love was almost tangible to the touch. I walked out of the room, and saw Mr. Finn sitting in the parlor reading his Bible.

"I said, 'Good morning, sir.'

"'You do not have to be so formal,' he said. 'We have quite a bit in common. Come in to the dining room. Your breakfast is almost ready.'

"He asked me to follow him and lead me to a small room in the back of the house. He set me in a chair in the middle of the room and said, 'Accepting Christ is only the beginning. You must be completely delivered.'

"He then spoke and called out the occult, false religion, spiritualism, guilt, fear schizophrenia, rebellion and bitterness. He commanded them all to go in Jesus's name.

"I felt my body begin to convulse, shake, and I began to cough and froth at the mouth. My whole body tensed up for what felt like an eternity. A loud yell then came out, and I was free. He then led me in a prayer to be filled with the Holy Ghost, and I felt clean.

"The man I would come to call father was delivered from the same spirits.

"He said, 'This is vital work in the kingdom of God. The strong man had to be called out of your body. You must stay consecrated unto the Lord to keep them from coming back and bringing back even more evil than they.

"After the deliverance we continued our coversation, then He said, 'Tell me about yourself, Michael?'

"'It is Tykellie. It means dark warrior in Latin.'

"Mr. Finn said, 'No. It is Michael. For you were born to be a great warrior for the kingdom of God.'

"'Whose God,' I asked.

"'The True God.' He bowed his head, crossed his arms over his chest, and said in the most reverent voice, 'My Lord and Savior JESUS CHRIST.'

He had tears in his eyes when he said it. I could tell how much his God meant to him, but why?

"'Where are those most excellent beings that were around you at the hotel?'

"'They are still here.

"'But I don't see them."

"'You saw them when you needed to. My God was simply getting your attention. Tell me about yourself.'

"I said, 'There really is not much to tell. All I have ever known is darkness from my birth. I have been trained in the black arts all of my life. I was not aware that such light existed until I saw Nina in the hotel lobby. Then I saw you with those magnificent beings standing on each side. They appeared to be mightier than anything I had ever seen before. I could not understand. When Nina told me that you were Christians, I did not understand. My father had Christians over to our home all of the time. He was very politically involved and told me that he had to keep a handle on the Christians. He never wanted them to be politically involved and he did. They all seemed to practice the separation of church and state. All of the legislations he wanted passed, because of their absence was notable. I watched as he manipulated political Christians to do his bidding consistently. I learned how to do this because of who I was to become. My father manipulated the entire town we were in by his spells and incantations over not only the politicians, civic leaders, but pastors of the churches as well. But none, absolutely none, had the power I saw with the both of you. How is that possible? My associates my whole life had been either warlocks, witches or demons. I was surprised when I woke up here, and my voices were not with me. My voices have been there since I can remember, but they turned on me at the final dedication and tried to destroy me. I don't understand what happened. Can you tell me? And why were you in a hotel when you have such a nice home here? Am I still in Africa?'

"'Okay, okay. Calm down,' Mr. Finn said. 'I have all of the answers you need but let me start from the very beginning.'

"He then told me his life story from the beginning. He started, 'I too was to be a warlock. A district warlock, and take over my father's position as he grew into a regional warlock.'

"'Really?' I asked.

"We sat down at the table, and Mrs. Finn brought us breakfast. She was a beautiful young woman with thick, curly long black hair. I could now see where Nina got her looks.

"Mr. Finn was a tall muscular man with black eyes and bronzish black skin. We looked much alike, but I could not figure out how. He said upon his final dedication he too had been prayed for by a Christian missionary in the jungles of Africa.

"'His name was Alexander Finn from Sweden. His whole life had been spent preaching the Gospel on the cotenant of Africa, and he said the Lord had specifically told him to pray for me. I was from the NINI tribe and my father was Chief Ubukatu.

"'No,' I said. 'The master warlock.'

"'He was not at that time. He was a district warlock over several tribes in the area. Their witch doctor, for lack of a better term. Mr. Finn had come into the village with two very large majestic beings. Their presence interrupted my meditation. So I came out of our hut. They came when all of the men were out hunting. Only women and children remained. He literally preached the Gospel to the entire village, and then gave me a New Testament Bible in our own language. I cherished mine. I would have been with the other men but my final dedication was to be that night and I had to stay and meditate. The arrival of Mr.

Finn broke my mediation, so I went out and listened. My voices warned me against him. They told me to stay in the hut, but my curiosity got the better of me. The light, that magnificent brilliant light. What power. I tried to talk to Mr. Finn but my voices were screaming so loudly that I could hardly stand. As I forced my way, they became fainter and fainter. I asked Mr. Finn who were those beings with you and where does this light come from. He said with great fervor it is the power of God. He grabbed and hugged me and simply said he would be praying for me. He finished preaching the gospel story and gave me a Bible, but no one else in the village seemed to see him. I took it back to my hut and things went on as usual, or so I thought. My voices came back and told me not to believe anything he said. That he was a liar. I wanted to believe them but there was a ring of truth in my very soul. I was very educated because of my position in the village so I could read with ease. The Bible was in my native tongue, I found out much later that this was a miracle, as none had been printed in my language. The Lord had made one especially for me. I sat and read the entire New Testament, and then dug a hole in the back of our hut, so father would not find it. I now understood, as if by some great revelation, there was a war going on between the Holy and the unholy. Good against evil. I realized that I was on the wrong side, but I did not know how to tell my father. He was a very harsh man, who accepted no questioning. I did not know my mother as well and everyone who came in to contact with me was scrutinized because of who I was about to become. Absolutely no outside influences were allowed. Mr. Finn should have never been able to penetrate that part of the jungle we were in, but he did. I read the little prayer in the back of the bible and accepted Jesus Christ as my Lord and Savior.'"

I noticed how emotional Mr. Mike became when he spoke the name.

"'Oh how wonderful it was. It was like soaring through the air. The peace came in like a river. The voices left permanently. I knew God face to face and I would give nothing to change that. But there was a dilemma. I had just turned 12 and was to be dedicated that night. I had no one except Jesus. When father and the others returned, I was confident that someone in the village would tell what had happened, but it was as if they did not see them. It really was my experience alone. Father came back and said nothing but come and led me out of the village, to the altar for final dedication, with other tribal witchdoctors' sons. I was the last to be dedicated, but the darkness that penetrated the other boys would not penetrate me. Father became very upset, and they meditated even more vehemently but it would not enter. At the end of the meeting, it was decided that I would be sacrificed on the altar. I was stripped naked, bound and placed on the altar. The fire was lit. I simply prayed, Jesus, into your hand I commend my spirit. Just like the Lord himself prayed on the cross according to the Bible that I had just read. Then, all of a sudden there was this brilliant light that shown all around me. I could see the fire through his wings but it did not burn me. That same peace I had received when I had accepted Jesus poured through my soul. I was safe. The being stood latterly inside the altar and placed his massive wings around me. I knew I was safe, then. I must have passed out, because I remember nothing else. The next morning, when I awoke, I rose off of the altar that had been totally consumed by fire and looked around. Everyone was gone. But I could tell by the position of the sun that it was still morning. I thanked the Lord for my life and looked and saw my clothes folded nicely on the ground with my sandals on top and, to my surprise, my New Testament. I got dressed and simply began walking. I knew I could not go back home, so I simply walked, trying to find my way out of the jungle. When I came to a clearing, I saw that missionary standing there. Missionary Finn. He was standing their like he was waiting for me. The exact spot where I was waiting for you. He walked over to me and simply said I will be your father now. He took me to his home town in Sweden and I became his son from that moment on. You see, I was his assignment just like you were mine, Michael. I loved Sweden, but felt the Lord calling me back to Africa after I reached adulthood. I go where I am sent and I was sent here for you.'

"'What is so special about that area where we were both to be sacrificed?'

"'Well, it is believed that is the spot where Satan was cast from glory into the earth. After causing a rebellion in heaven. Satan could not destroy God, or become God, so he rebelled. When he saw how God loved man, he decided he would try and hurt God by hurting his creation. Mr. Finn, now my father, was a devout Christian who loved the Lord with all of his might. He was a wonderful man, full of the Holy Ghost and powerful in the Lord. He was very loving and soft spoken. Most people in our community called him Father, even though he was a fairly young man of about 40. Mr. Finn had met me exactly where I met you, about 30 years ago. This ritual has been going on for hundreds of years. It started when a young African prince who had been rejected by his family and tribe because of his looks, he was born with a growing tumor on his face that had repelled his family and his people. It was because of his looks he could not be king. The tumor was about the size of a basketball. By the time he reached puberty, the tumor on his face was believed to have weighted by about 30 pounds. By the time he reached young adulthood, 40 pounds. Being king required beauty of the face, even though he was a brilliant scholar, articulate and quick witted, he could not be king. It would actually go to his younger brother. One day he wandered into a cave and heard voices speaking to him, telling him that they could make him beautiful and ruler if he would dedicate himself to it and worship it. Satan longs to be worshiped and will offer anything to get it.

He agreed and sacrificed hundreds of animals in that cave. It was after that he walked out of the cave, fully cured in body. The tumor had literally fallen off of his face, but he was horribly plagued in his spirit. It is said that he was possessed by Satan himself. He was made King and lead his people into horrible abominable acts of violence. He began to conquer other tribes and require their children to be dedicated to Satan in that very cave. The cave eventually eroded away over time, but the land was thought to be too spiritual to place anything like buildings or infrastructure, so altars of mortar and wood were built once a year. As the king reign grew, he became convinced by Satan that he would be forever young in this life and reign with him in Hell. So a plan was devised to carry Satan's plot throughout the world, so each tribe conquered was given an area to subdue for their master. It grew from Africa across the waters into Asia, Europe, Australia, to the seven continents of the world. So that now children are bred to take over the regions for Satan. You and I were such children. Same mothers, different fathers. I found my mother when I grew into a man, and lead her to Christ. She was an old woman and had been put out once she reached menopause because she could not have children anymore. The Lord led me to the church one rainy evening. I heard someone hitting on the door. I looked out, and there was this old woman outside screaming trying to get in. She yelled out for help. I opened the door and helped her in. It was at that time that she changed and began to spit and curse. Then she would come back to herself and yell out for help. The deacons were having a meeting that evening and came to see the commotion. I recognized the enemy and commanded it to come out. But it was stubborn. She had a legion of demons in her, and they all began to cry out she is ours. She has given herself freely and she is ours. I then heard her cry again. The deacons and I gathered around her and began to worship and praise God. She then threw herself on the floor and froth at the mouth, then I spoke the name, and I could feel and see the power of God go out from me and hit her. She was holding her breath, and I then saw hundreds of demons, black, scaly, and hideous, fly out of her. She then collapsed. I then spoke the name and I could feel the power of God encompass me. She looked like she was holding her breath again. She then collapsed and I alone saw them leave her body. Hundreds and hundreds had possessed her over the years and had destroyed her. We picked her up and sent for the missionaries to come in and help get her cleaned up. After they cleaned her up, changed her clothes and put shoes on her feet, she was given food and a place to rest. We all rejoiced that Satan lost another one. She came back into the sanctuary and told the deacons, missionaries and I the most disturbing story we had ever heard. She said she was taken from her family when she was about four, and taught the dark arts until she was a teenager. At that time, she was given in marriage to a regional warlock and had at least eight children with him. She had lost several in pregnancy or at birth, but she knew she had to have had at least eight live births because she heard their cries. She was now 65, and could no longer have children, so she was put out of the coven because there was no use for her any more. She said she had no place to go. She had been dedicated to Satan and he was all she knew, but when they put her out, she said she remembered her mother told her once about a savior named JESUS. The moment she thought it she said she felt great convulsing pressure. She heard loud screams and moans telling her to stop, and that they were going to kill her. She said she was born in India, but had been all over the world. She was told she would be rewarded, but she was not. She was kicked out and dumped in Africa once she could no longer have children. She was told she was not worthy to be sacrificed which was her desire, and she said she knew no one in Africa and since she was only four when she was abducted, she knew no one anywhere. She had been living in the jungle in a hut she had built all alone. She said she felt driven to the church, but repulsed by it at the same time. She said she felt as if she had several different personalities, but they were too strong for her to handle. When she recited the incantations she was taught to ease her mind, it only made things worse for her. So she said she had nowhere to go. She said she decided that this would be the last day she lived like an animal, and she fought to get to the church today, with a prayer in her heart. If Jesus is real. He will help me. Thank you, thank you for saving my life. I explained to her, yes Jesus is real and she had been delivered but that she had to accept Him as savior or those same demons that were just cast out would come back, and worse. She agreed and became a Christian that very day. She was allowed to live in the small home behind the church. It was clean and mildly furnished. I would see her often because she attended the church regularly. I told her she had the most beautiful eyes they were black and she had coper skin. She said you look just like I did at your age. I was unusual. Born in India with black eyes. Her great grandfather had black eyes. She said she could remember her mother telling her she was special because of that and it always comforted her knowing she was special. She continued and said I remember my father was African American. I cannot prove it but I believe you could possibly be my son. All of the children I gave birth to I was not allowed to see but if they were my children, I knew they would have my great, great grandfather's trait of black eyes. I found out later it was a condition called Anirion that affects about five percent of the Indian population. The eyes stood out because our skin is coper, regardless of what the father looked like. Since no records of these births were recorded, I asked if she remember the man she was married to. She said he was a regional warlock. He was a harsh and cold man, but so was she. They had but one goal, to serve Satan with their whole hearts. She remembered he died screaming for help. Thats when doubt began to creep in. If they were going to rule in Hell, wouldn't their death be peaceful and rewarding. She never forgot that and it caused her to live in fear, but she kept serving blindly. She became good friends with my family and would visit often. She died 7 years ago, but I told her I would do all I could to find her children and bring them to Christ, and I have. You are the 8th and last, so I have completed my assignment. We both get our eyes from our mother. You were the last child she gave birth to before she went into menopause, and we prayed together for you, and all of her children. She was taught by baring children for Satan, that she would live forever and secure her place as co ruler in the kingdom of Hell, but Satan uses people until they are nothing. Then he drags their poor souls into Hell. We look alike because I believe we are probably brothers. I remembered felling strangely sad and happy at the same time. Sad in that I was not conceived in love, but I had a real family and that seemed to comfort all of my very deep, deep wounds.'"

It was at that time that Mr. Mike's daughter came in and said, "It is time for rest."

Mr. Mike looked up and simply smiled. it was after 7:30 p.m.

I did not realize I had been there so long. I reluctantly got up and said, "I will see you in the morning. How about 7 a.m.?"

He said, "How about eight a.m.? I have to get my walk in."

"Eight a.m. will be fine," I said. I left most of my equipment in the house but I took my tape recorder with me.

What a fascinating life he has had. I rode back silently, thinking and rethinking how such a story like this has never been told. When I arrived at the hotel, I thought long and hard about the things Mr. Mike had spoken about battles and warfare, right before our very eyes.

Then I remembered my great grandfather, when I was young, used to speak of such things. Then my grandfather and father alike.

I had no desire to be in the ministry, so I did not put a whole lot of emphasis on it. But I began to remember with great clarity the battle stories, and how much they loved God.

Chapter 3

I was a Christian. I prayed. I believed. I thought they were simply trying to coerce me into the family business. That of ministry, and I was not going to have it.

I wanted to be a journalist my whole life, and that is what I was going to be. But I think my life has now come full circle. The very thing I ran from as a child, I had come right back into.

When we arrived at the hotel, I prepared for bed, said my prayers, got into bed, and closed my eyes. I had the most peaceful sleep I had ever had. It was like I was doing what I was born to do, and I somehow knew it. I can't explain it, but I just knew, and the peace was wonderful.

I thought the decision I had made as a child growing up in the church had protected me from all of my bad decisions in adulthood, but I was beginning to see there was much, much more to the Christian walk than I had realized.

The next morning, the wake-up call came at 5:30 a.m., as per my request.

I pounced out of the bed, into the shower, grabbed my things, and was out of the hotel waiting by 6 a.m.

It was then that it dawned on me that the driver would not be here until 6:30, so I went in and had some breakfast.

The hotel manager walked over to me and said, "So. How is the interview going with Mr. Mike?"

This man was literally known by everyone.

"Wonderful," I said. "How do you know him?"

"He and my grandfather were very good friends. They were both in the ministry together.

That was strange. I always thought the ministry would be somehow boring, but in speaking with Mr. Mike, I began to remember more and more the excitement my relatives would show when they spoke of battles in the heavens.

How could I have forgotten all of that?

The manager said, "I had forgotten as well, until I came of age."

He was about 30 years my senior.

Just then, Zahede asked, "Are you ready?"

"Yes," I said.

We walked out of the hotel into a most beautiful day. The sky was blue with very few clouds. The city was still somewhat quiet and I could hear the birds chirping. The natural sounds became more prominent as we left the confines of the city.

I could hear elephants, lions, gazelles, zebras, and monkeys. There was an orchestra in the jungle at this hour. How wonderful.

When we arrived at Mr. Mikes home, I walked slowly up the sidewalk because I enjoyed watching the beautiful butterflies flutter.

What a beautiful home, I thought. And what a beautiful life, too.

When I arrived at the front door a sign said come to the back.

Just as I walked around the porch to the back, I saw Mr. Mike walking on to the porch.

"I got out late this morning because of the rain but I feel great." He was dripping wet. I assumed from the rain. He said, "No. It's from the walk. I walk two miles a day.

I thought. How is it possible a 115-year-old man walks 2 miles a day?

Absolutely no one in the States will believe this, so I got a couple of pictures.

He said, "I am going to take a quick shower, make yourself at home."

I followed him back to his study and prepared my equipment, changed tapes, and checked audio. The whole nine yards.

This has got to be Pulitzer Prize material, I thought as I prepared for the interview, and looked around at the beautiful study.

I figured while I wait, I will look at the books to see what type of literature a 115-year-old man reads. But these looked like originals. As I looked, I noticed that they did not have an author's signature. Or a publishing date. Or anything.

It looked like every book I touched was an original. I picked up about 10.

I decided to read one. However, it appeared to be a book in a sequence so I had a brilliant idea. I would go to the first book in the library.

Sure enough, it was the beginning and the story was about Mr. Mike and his friends and their adventures.

Just then, Mr. Mike walked in, full of vigor and noticed me reading.

"Have you read much?"

"No. just got started. Are all of these books about you?"

"Mostly," he said. "I made a promise that one day I would have all of them published, before I went home to be with the Lord, that day is soon arriving. Would you like a cup of tea this morning?"

"No. I have already had breakfast."

He sat down with a cup of tea Ms. Dottie had brought him and noticed it smelled like hot apple pie.

"It smells great," I told him.

"Are you sure you don't want a cup?"

I again declined, wanting desperately for him to continue his story.

"Now where were we?" Mr. Mike said. I started the equipment and sat in the large leather chair right next to him. "As I was saying, Satan has his people in the earth. These are people that have been dedicated to him through ceremony, or a decision, to do his bidding by perpetuating laws to remove God's word from mankind.

"Some are used by him totally unknowingly, but there will be no excuse, because every man has a conscience. We all know what is right and wrong. We simply choose what suits us for that moment."

After stating that, Mr. Mike continued his story, "I continued to live in Africa with my new family and went to school there. These were probably the most care free days of my life. Nina and I were best friends, something I never had. I made more friends in the local school I was attending. We played all types of games after school. My favorite was cricket. I fancied myself a professional, and I was the best in the small town we lived in.

"I made excellent grades, and thought maybe one day I would go to college and study like father did in Switzerland. He only said that we would see what the Lord has for me. You see, Father had an earned Ph.D. in Theology, and was very skilled in different languages. He spoke three fluently. African (several dialects), Swede, and English.

"Father taught Nina and I these languages as well within a year. I had the Swedish language down, and most of the African dialects, and could read and write it fluently.

"I enjoyed my life so very much, I thought I was enjoying a little taste of Heaven on earth. Father had always been a brilliant scholar, and had the largest church in Africa. Unheard of in that day, but he had over 2,000 members. Every Sunday they would come into a one room mud building. There were always people in the courtyard that could not get in.

"There were all types of miracles that took place. Cancers fell off of bodies, blinded eyes were opened, the deaf would hear, the lame would walk. Father was so consecrated to GOD, that his nick name was Father Elijah.

"He was nicknamed after Elijah, because in the Bible, Elijah asked God to hold back the rain for 3 ½ years and he did, and whatever father asked God to do, God did it. Father was never afraid, and enjoyed his ministry very much, but always prayed that God would have his perfect, not permissive will done in his life.

"One spring day as we all sat down for dinner. Father said he received a call from an old professor in America and that he was on the board of a church that needed a new pastor. But I said, 'Father we are so happy here.'

"He responded, 'Yes we are, but true happiness is being in the perfect will of GOD. The church is located in Perfect, California.'

"How could this be? that is where I was originally from. It was the exact same city.

"'But Father,' I said. 'I do not wish to go back to that area. It holds nothing but pain and loneliness for me.'

"'Not any more,' he said. 'You are a new creature in Christ, and no weapon formed against you can prosper.'

"I was immediately comforted when father spoke the word.

"We began packing the next morning. Father turned the church over in Africa to the assistant pastor and said he did not know when, but he hoped to return one day.

"There was an elaborate ceremony to install the assistant pastor and to pray for God's will in Father's life in his new mission field.

"I cried because I really wanted to live out the rest of my life in this wonderfully peaceful village, where people loved and respected each other. It was so peaceful that we slept with our doors open. We could walk the streets at any hour in our town of Peaceful Africa, which is what it was nicknamed, which was really a small town in Nairobi.

"If anyone was hurting the whole town would come to their rescue. It was a safe haven for Christians who fled from the radical Muslims. For some reason, the radical Muslims were never allowed to enter, but the peaceful ones were able to enter Peaceful Africa.

"Father said because we had dedicated this land to The Lord and lived according to the word, the Lord would protect anyone who came there.

"One day, while Father and I were out walking, he said, 'Look.'

"And I saw all around Peaceful were these towering Angels, they stood as tall as the trees and had pure white wings trimmed in gold. They had on gold sashes, and powerful looking golden swords in their hands. Their skin was like bronze, and their faces like lightening.

"Father said, 'The earth is the Lord's. The world and they that dwell therein. But Satan comes and attempts to steal the land by using man to do his bidding in the earth. Do you understand son? Your job is to take back what Satan has stolen from man, and always remember all the glory always goes to God, and God loves mankind regardless of what they have done.'

"Father could see my concern and simply said, 'The victory is already ours. He can never leave us or forsake us. Hold on to that. You have the true God now, and no weapon formed against you will prosper.'

"We sold our simple quaint little home and moved. When we neared America, Father motioned to me and said, 'Look, the principality over America.'

"I saw large dark, smoky clouds and a powerful creature sitting on what looked like a large silver throne. It was muscular in form, like a powerful man but had the horns of a goat and the face like a bear. It wore jewels around its arms and chest. Its eyes were deep blood red. He sat there as if he were ruling the country.

"I asked, 'Father, what is that?'

"Nina and mother saw nothing but sunshine, but mother knew never to interrupt father when the Lord was reveling something to him, so she simply sat quietly, as did Nina, and prayed.

"Father said, 'Behold the principality that rules America.'

"I saw a name on it, and it said DECEPTION. Deception was the ruling principality in America. In Africa, even though I never saw it, Father said the ruling principality was False Religion.

"The fact that God had revealed the ruling principality to me let father know that this was my battle ground. That is why father had been constantly training me while I was in Africa. I literally knew the Bible in three different languages, front and backwards.

"Father said, 'This country is a democracy. Therefore, Satan has to keep them in a constant state of deception. For example, the idea of freedom of speech a wonderful concept that was agreed upon by their founding fathers. Satan has taken the right from their preachers, so they cannot preach the whole gospel from their pulpits, making Christianity ineffective and communities weak. Under the word of choice, innocent children are being slaughtered daily. People have been deceived that the child in the womb is not a child, that it has no feelings, no emotions, it is but a blob they are deceived so the people, including Christians, vote pro-abortion politicians because they have no alternatives. True Christians simply are not running for any offices. Alternate lifestyle is what sexual perversion is being called. The people have been deceived to believe that people are born this way, when in actuality, it is Satan who has perverted them into thinking this way. You see, Satan comes in when they are very young. Lack of proper authority, illicit pictures, rape, generational curses play a part in this perversion. These circumstances are so persuasive, his set ups are so good that they believe it. You see, the blood is needed for protection against the enemy. They have been deceived to believe that the sexually perverted person can't change just like a black man can't change his skin color. But it is a trick of the enemy. They need deliverance, and God is standing ready to do so if any ask him. He loves them so much, but they too are so deceived, that they cannot see the truth. They attempt to serve GOD in this lifestyle and it's like mixing water with oil, and it will not mix. Children are not allowed to pray in schools because they have been deceived to believe that God should not be a part of a young child's life. They might be influenced by religion and contaminated somehow. Separation of church and state is a farce. You cannot separate one from the other. Their entire government has been built on the Bible, and now they want to take away the very thing that gives them liberty. They are litigating right now to have God actually taken off of their money, and out of their courts. Not realizing that if they turn off the light, that darkness automatically comes in. All of this has been influenced by the regional warlock in this area.'

"I remember feeling such shame, but Father recognized it, and said, 'You have nothing to be ashamed of. You were but a child and taught that wrong was right. God has delivered you for this purpose. We have a great work to do for the Lord.

"'We,' I asked.

"'Yes. We,' he said. 'All under the banner of freedom. Satan is destroying this people by perverting their own constitution. Deception. They actually have books that are published to refute the word of God, and they make those books mandatory reading for school age children. Children are not allowed to speak the name of the Lord in schools. Does this seem sane to you?'

"'No, Father. It does not,' I said.

"'Deception. That is why there is so much darkness over the land. They are deceived, and we are going where the 20th regional warlock has taken a strong hold on the country by manipulating the political system there.'

I continued to look while father spoke, and there were what looked like lesser demons bringing reports to Deception the principality.

"They were smaller and less jeweled, or not jeweled at all. All of their appearances were horribly disfigured.

"'What are they reporting' I asked Father.

"'They are putting their people in their political offices so that they can totally deceive this people, and destroy this nation. Satan has been successful with destroying nations as powerful, if not more powerful than, America in the past. Greece. Rome. Babylon. The list goes on. Right now, in America what use to be right is now wrong and what use to be wrong is now right. That is why the regional warlock is fighting so hard to get the Bible out of public life, schools, court rooms, etc.

"'The imps are sent to take over each political system from the board of education to the Presidents Office of the United States of America. America is responsible for more missionary work than any other country in the world today and Satan hates her. Even when she was becoming a country slavery took hold and was a stronghold in this country for centuries. Satan realizes that America cannot be destroyed from without so has to be corrupted from within. Slavery is to this day a horrible blight on this country's history. You see, there is a hierarchy of evil. Satan imitates God's chain of command on every level. But don't worry that battle is already won.'

"Just as father said that, I saw blue sky again and sun shine. I thought this is what the people of America see. They are not even aware that they have been deceived.

"How sad, how sad. To live in such a wonderful country and pushing the very thing away that gave them that beauty, the Bible. How sad I thought.

"When we arrived, a man by the name of Mr. Wells met us and we eventually called him the Professor, because he taught college for more than 40 years in Switzerland before he retired to America, where he was born. He taught Father through college. He was an older gentleman, slightly balding with grey and black hair on the sides. He was very distinguished looking.

"When he saw Father, he rushed and hugged him. They embraced like they were brothers. We found out later that the Professor also had a Ph.D. in Theology but never had met the Lord until Father was his student, and held his feet to the fire regarding the Bible.

"He had taught for more than 20 years at that time, and had lost everything, including his faith. He was an alcoholic who had a horrible addiction to explicit pictures. It was Father who helped him realize that, and brought him into a relationship with the Lord.

"The Professor never forgot how Father helped him. Father helped him bring his family together, and to see that God really did love him. It was because of this that he never forgot Father, and always sent him birthday gifts and magazines of wonderful homes every year.

"Father fancied himself a builder, as well, and he enjoyed looking at the beautiful homes in other countries, and building on additions to our home. The Professor knew this and would send magazines of such homes as often as he could. He loved him like a son.

"After his retirement, he always wanted to move back to the United States, so he did. He retired in Perfect with his wife.

"We exited the airport and put our things in the Professor's car. He began to tell the whole family how he had struggled to find a decent church in this area. One that preached the true Gospel. He said he went to over 125 churches in the area, of all denominations, and they were all like social clubs. No power.

"Until he met Pastor Anderson. He was a powerful preacher that would not waver when it came to the gospel. He was a man born without much and had done time in prison for murder. He came from a broken home where his mother was a drug addict and his mother's boyfriends took advantage of him from the age of five until he was 15. It was at that time that he killed a man for trying to take advantage of him yet one more time. He was a juvenile that spent 20 years in juvenile homes and in prison.

"The pastor of the prison befriended him and led him to the Lord. When he got out of prison, he had nowhere to go, so he came to Perfect, California to be with the pastor who had become a real father to him.

"He had had no children, and willed the church that he started to him on his death bed. It was a small church, of about 50 members. He had loved the Lord with his whole heart and the Lord had shown him that this boy, who Satan had tried to destroy as a child would, do great exploits for the Lord one day.

"Pastor Anderson, who was totally sold out to God for delivering him from such a horrible lifestyle, had a chance to look into the other world. The world of the supernatural. He could always see the enemy coming, just did not know how to defeat him. He could see how people were taken over by dark images, and how they would cause the humans to do their bidding. He had been delivered of more than 100 demons himself. Every time he was taken advantage of, something evil would enter him and stay. He hated with great passion but did not know how to stop it, until Pastor Liddey came into his life through his small ministry.

"He explained that in this world, we wrestle not against mankind, but against powers and principalities in high places. After he heard that sermon, he sought out Pastor Liddey to explain to him how to be delivered, because he knew the desires he had were perverted because he had been taking advantage of so often. He was possessed and was helpless to defend himself. He was involved in all types of perversion.

"He accepted Christ as a defense, but came to a true understanding of who he was and how much God truly loved him immediately. Once delivered, he was on fire for God and nothing could stop him. When he took the Pastoral ship of Mount Zion Baptist Church, the other pastors in the town did not care to associate with him very much. He was too radical for their taste.

"But as Father always said, 'If much is forgiven He returns much love.'

"His church was growing in leaps and bounds. Drug addicts were being delivered. violent people were becoming peaceful. Families that had be ripped apart by Satan were brought back together.

"He was never silent about sin in the community. He staged sit ins at the abortion clinics. He would stage protests against adult material stores. He fought for prayer during graduation services at schools. The list went on.

"He had told his testimony so many times in the city that everyone knew it front and backwards.

"He was now almost 90.

"The Professor and Pastor Anderson became good friends and the pastor told the Professor that he was looking for a successor. He had no children and he did not think his current associate minister had the stamina to handle the battle the Lord had shown him that was about to come to pass when he left this world.

"He said that he had been praying and fasting for more than eight years. He knew God had a man. He just did not know exactly who. 'I told him I believed that man was you when I told him who you were, your name what you looked like what your educational background was and he said immediately with great enthusiasm that is the man.'

"Apparently he had a dream and the Lord had reveled Father to him in great detail.

"He said, 'You were the man God had revealed to him that was destined to be the Under Shepard of this flock.'

"As we continued on, Father asked how he was able to get a home in America for such a small amount of cash he sent him. The Professor said something very strange to my Father.

"He said, 'There had been some rumors about the home which is why I got it for such a wonderfully low price. No one has lived there for more than 20 years. It's a beautiful home. The church members have pitched in and cleaned and furnished it for you. But there have been times where I almost felt as if I was being watched while I was in it. But knowing you I am positive that it will not be a problem at all.'

"You see, the professor taught theology for a very long time and had totally accepted Christ, but he would say some things I simply prefer not to see.

"'It has not been officially dedicated to the Lord yet. Pastor Anderson has been so busy lately that he has not made it over there yet. But he told me since you are a man of God not to worry. No weapon formed against him will prosper.'

"Father smiled and said, 'I am confident we all will be just fine.'

"As we continued, I began to look up. I remembered vividly what the town looked like, even though I was forbidden to ever leave the yard. I would look at Perfect through the telescope in my old father's library. All I was ever allowed to do was look down from our home on high in the mountains. I never came down.

"It was then I saw it. My old home. There it was, high above the city, dark and cold looking, a flash of remembrance came across my mind and I became afraid once again. Father seemed to sense it, and simply said out loud, 'God has not given us a spirit of fear, but of love, power, and of sound mind.'

"I was comforted immediately. As we drove down the streets, I saw a movie theater that had a film on the marquee with the title of *The Exorcism of John Byoue*,

"'Are you kidding,' Nina asked the Professor. 'What kind of entertainment could that possible be?'

"'Here in the United States it is the number one film.'

"She asked father how and why.

"He spoke very clearly, and said, 'In every nation, Satan has a plan for destruction. In this country it is through their entertainment. Movie theaters, music, art, print, internet, and games. Not realizing, they draw Satan to themselves. He comes but to steal, kill and destroy and here that is how he gets into their homes and destroys the family. The family is the foundation of every civilized community, and Satan has attacked it in this country with both barrels. A lot of times the father who should be protecting the homes from such filth bring it in themselves and subject their own children to demonic attack. Or the family does not have a priest to protect the home because the father is not there. In some cases, they have tried to rearrange the family totally. We have our work cut out for us.'

"It was then we pulled up to our new home. It was a beautiful stone brick, two story home with a large yard. All of the homes here looked very rich and beautiful, they dwarfed our old home, even with Fathers additions.

"When we opened the door, The Professor's wife was in the kitchen cooking. She was an older woman with white hair that was tied up in a neat little bun. She had on a very frilly apron that fit her close, showing her very petit frame. Her name was Falona. We all called her Mrs. Professor.

'What a wonderful smell,' she greeted us all with hugs and said, 'Welcome to America. Please come in to your new home, I and some of the ladies from the church decorated it, how do you like it?'

"'It's beautiful,' mother said.

"'Come. Come. Let's eat. I will show you around after dinner, I am sure you are starving after such a long trip.'

"We walked into the dining room and it was right out of one of the magazines I had seen that the Professor had sent Father. It had a very low hanging chandelier with crystal droplets trimmed in gold. And the dining room set was absolutely beautiful. there was a curio cabinet, a buffet ,a China cabinet, and an octagon shaped table all in rich cherry wood."

Mr. Mike then paused, and said, "I inherited my dinning set from those furnishings. What do you think about it?"

I said, "Yes. It's exceptionally beautiful."

It was one of the first things I noticed about Mr. Mikes home. Apparently his family had willed it to him, and he had taken great care of it.

He then continued, "I remember vividly what was most appealing to Nina and I was the food. We had roast turkey with all of the trimmings. It was wonderful. Father normally ate very little, but for this occasion I actually saw him take seconds. Father and the Professor were great friends, and it would have been a tremendous insult if Father had not eaten well. So ever gracious he did and really enjoyed catching up with the Professor.

"After dinner, Mrs. Professor and Mother went for a tour around the home. Nina and I followed. The home had been furnished. It was absolutely beautiful, and I actually had my own room. The bedrooms were very basic. There was a bed dresser, night stand, lamp, and it had the most unusual comforter I had ever seen. It had weaved in gold print 'Prince of the Lord' on it. The women of the church had made the comforters with special stitching. Nina's said 'Maiden of the Lord' on hers. My room was blue and hers was pink.

"I was marvelously overjoyed at how abundantly the Lord had blessed me and my wonderful new family. I will come back in the morning to take you to meet Pastor Anderson."

Chapter 4

"That evening, I told Father that while I was in my room alone I felt a presence but I could not put my finger on it. It was very familiar though.

He said. So did I.

"Mother and Nina had gone with Mrs. Professor and her friend to her home, to pick up Father and Mother's comforter the church women were finishing it up, and they wanted to make sure they had it there first night in their new home.

"Father said, 'We must dedicate this home to the Lord now. It is apparent that Satan has stolen here once, and we do not want to give him another opportunity.'

"Father began to pray, and I could hear things rattling.

"Father then stopped and spoke into nothingness, 'Show yourself.'

"And this thing which looked as if it were covered with maggots and roaches appeared. It was a spirit of Lust. It smelled awful. Even more awful than anything I had smelled in Africa. Thick black and green smoke came from it. Its eyes were squinting.

"It hovered over the floor and said, 'This is my home!'

"Father did not even respond to it. He simply took the authority he had been given by God.

"I looked and saw gold bands bind it and then it was sucked into a black whole that simply appeared in the ceiling, and disappeared after Lust was sucked into it.

"Immediately the air felt clean. Father took the holy oil and anointed all of the doors and windows in the home. It was at that time that Mother and Nina came home.

"We all marveled out loud at the wonderful gifts we had received from the Lord. We gave thanks to the Lord and retired to bed. It had been a wonderfully exhausting day.

"Right before I went into my room, Father said, 'Now son. The battle is waging and you are anointed by God to do great exploits in his name. Remember that and sleep well.'

"I went to sleep that night, wondering what type of exploits I could do for Him who had done so much for me. I only hoped that I would be ready when the time came.

"Fear was no longer a part of my life. I learned to look evil right in the face and take authority over it the name of JESUS, because HE alone has all power and nothing can stand against him.

"I would live a Godly life, so that God and God alone would get the glory from my life."

"Lunch time," I heard.

Mr. Mike smiled and said, "Race you to the porch."

That is where Mrs. Dottie would serve lunch. She would eat with us, but would never allow us to talk about the article. She just wanted to talk about me for some odd reason.

I had to admit, I thought it was an interesting coincidence that both Mr. Mike and I had lived in the same part of the country at one time or the other. I told him it was possible that maybe he knew some of my relatives. He simply smiled and said possibly.

Mrs. Dottie had prepared some type of zebra roll which tasted surprisingly like chicken, with a small salad and tea. It was wonderful as usual.

It started to rain, so after lunch we retired back to the study.

Mr. Mike asked, as he normally did after a break, where were we, even though he always knew. This man had a sharp memory. It was still amazing to me that he was as old as he was. I simply kept quiet and let him tell me his life story.

"Oh yes," he said. "The next day the family got up early and had breakfast. The Professor came by, and brought what looked like a new car.

"'It is yours,' he said. The professor fancied himself a restorer of old things and he restored this car for our family.

"'Now I will have to get a license,' Father said with a smile.

"We all traveled to see Pastor Anderson. We went to his very modest but neat home. Pastor Anderson opened the door. He barley looked 50 years old.

We entered the home and Pastor Anderson embraced Father, and said, 'You have a difficult road to climb. I have taken it as far as I can. Now, it's your turn. I am more than confident you will be successful.'

"His wife was 83 years old and had passed away just 3 months ago. They had been married for 62 years. I heard him tell father that he missed her and felt the Lord calling him home, as well, once he had his successor in place.

"Pastor Anderson said, 'Please look at the history of the church that your family will be inheriting. My wife kept very meticulous records of church activities.'

"He and father left the room and went into a small parlor and spoke.

"Nina, mother and I were going through all of the photo albums he had underneath his massive coffee table. It was solid oak with a large shelf underneath. There must have been 20, very neatly put together photo albums, placed in order of year. He had pictures of himself when he and his wife were very young.

"He had pictures of the dedication of the church, anniversaries, birthdays, the list goes on. His life was literally detailed in these photo albums.

"Just as I looked up, I saw Pastor Anderson hand father something.

"He hugged him, and said, 'I will see you tomorrow morning in church.'

"We arose early the next morning so that we could attend Sunday school. It was a medium sized church, but was almost packed to capacity in Sunday school.

"What must the service be like, I thought.

"According to the plaque on the wall, I saw a capacity of 800. There had to already be 500 people in that building in Sunday school.

"My Sunday school class alone had about 75 people in it. They all seemed to drink the word in, as if their very lives depended on it.

"The worship afterward was very spirit filled. So much so that demons began to manifest right in the service. One boy I took note of. He seemed to stand out. He was a little muffed up. He was in dirty jeans, and a dirty denim jacket. Even though I sat diagonally behind him I noticed a tattoo of an eagle on his hand, when he scratched his head. He had a very poignant odor coming from him. He was a big guy. Very muscular build. He appeared to be in a great deal of pain, I noticed. As praise and worship continued, he began to vomit and swear. The people simply moved away, and the Deacons came over I was in a perfect spot to see exactly what happened.

"This was a stubborn one I thought. It was so disruptive that Pastor Anderson moved quietly over to him. But I could hear his voice. It was thick with power. He asked its name.

"It growled and said, 'He is mine!'

"Pastor said to the boy, 'You tell it to go.'

"I heard the boy say, 'Go!' Then a loud screech came out of the boy and he went limp.

Pastor Anderson went ahead and completed the deliverance by calling out the strongman called addictive compulsive.

"They all came out with a yell. It was immediately over when the boy told it to go.

"The boy was taken to the back, cleaned up, and brought back out when the Pastor got up to speak.

"He actually looked clean. He had on a suit with a tie. It did not even look like the same boy but, I recognized the tattoo on his hand.

"Pastor Anderson began his sermon. It was absolutely wonderful. I still remember it. Matthew, 5th chapter. The Beatitudes. My favorite part was, 'The pure in heart shall see God.'

"Oh, how I wanted to see God face to face.

"This type of service was the norm at Pastor Anderson's church. Which is why this church had grown in leaps and bounds.

"The power of God was being manifested every Sunday. At prayer meetings, at choir rehearsals, and Bible studies. This was a true New Testament Church, much like our church in Africa.

"We would be right at home here, I thought.

"Pastor Anderson stood up. He gave the message and over 50 people came to give their lives to Christ. They did not just walk down the aisle. They came running with tear stained faces and with tears in their eyes. What a wonderful church this was.

"After service, Pastor Anderson, Father, and I took the boy home.

"Apparently last night, when the boy was walking, he was caught in a torrential thunderstorm, so he ran into the church. Pastor Anderson just happened to be there late.

"The boy looked hungry. Pastor Anderson gave him his lunch, and allowed him to sleep there, overnight in the nurse's room.

"When the boy awoke Pastor Anderson had brought him breakfast and a suit of clothes the next morning. The boy was so grateful that he decided to stay for service at Pastors request, but he did not want to wear the suit of clothes. So he did not, at first.

"When I was introduced to him, Pastor began what seemed like a list of names in introducing me to the young man.

"The young man said, 'you can call me Bud.'

"I thanked him, and asked him how old he was. He said 13. We were the same age but he was at least 30lbs heavier and 3 inches taller than I.

"Pastor Anderson wanted me to go with father, and one of the deacons of the church, to take Bud home. When we pulled up to his home, I felt very sad for him. His home looked like and old abandon shack. There was trash in the yard, and huge patches of dirt. Just filthy. The windows had no curtains, and the porch was broken in almost two pieces.

"It was a small white house that needed much repair. Nevertheless, we all walked up to the porch and Pastor Anderson knocked, but no one came to the door.

"Bud said he is probably still high and passed out in his room. Pastor Anderson said to Bud, 'With your permission.'

"He took two small pieces of steel, and placed them in the key hole, and the door opened like it was a key.

"Paster Anderson smiled and simply said, 'I have not always been a pastor.'

"The house was totally trashed. There was filth everywhere, so Pastor Anderson asked me to wait outside with Bud, it was then the deacon came running out.

"They had found Bud's father in a pool of vomit. He had no pulse.

"'Go next door and ask the neighbors if you can call the ambulance.'

"Both Bud and I did so. We did not know all of this until afterward, but Bud's father had died. While Father and Pastor waited for the ambulance they began to pray. God had intervened and by the time the ambulance arrived, Bud's father was alive and visibly shaken.

"He kept saying, 'No. No! Please, don't let them take me back!'

"He repeated that for hours in the hospital until they could get him calmed down. Father and I left, and Bud went home with Pastor Anderson and stayed until his father was well. He asked us to meet him back at the hospital the next morning, at about 9:00.

"Father agreed. I could not figure out why they wanted me there, but they did.

"So, the next morning we came back to the hospital. Bud's father was now coherent and thanked them for pulling him out of that horrible place.

"'Tell me about it,' Pastor Anderson said.

"He wanted Bud and I to be there.

"He said, 'I was being dragged by creatures who kept saying we have him now. It was smoky and dark almost dingy. Things were tearing at my flesh and I was in immense pain. I cried out, but no one cared. I felt no love. Just hate, suffering, and pain. I sadly knew that this is where I should be, because of my life on Earth. I saw huge snakes, and man size bat-like creatures. I felt trapped until I heard my name called. At that point I was literally torn from those things, and found myself back on the bathroom floor. OHHHHHHH!!!!!! I never want to go their again.'

"Pastor said, 'You do not have to if you accept the Savior in your life.'

"'How? How? How do I do that?'

"Pastor simply unfolded the gospel in such a way that even a child could understand it. How the Christ had come in the form of a man named Jesus to purchase mankind's authority back from Satan, after Adam had relinquished it to him in the Garden of Eden. And now because of the blood He shed on Calvary, every human being has the right to Heaven.

"It was then that Bud's father, Mr. Paul, who we called him by his first name, tried to say yes, but felt as if he was being chocked. He coughed and gagged. He had no voice.

"Pastor Anderson simply said, 'By the authority of Christ,' and spoke the name with such power that the things let go of his throat and he was set free. From that day on, he never did drugs or took so much as a drink or a cigarette. He had seen Hell, and he was not going back.

"Mr. Paul stayed in the hospital for a total of 10 days. The doctors had expected there to be some type of reaction to the lack of drugs. But Mr. Paul simply read his Bible daily and prayed all of the time. When it was obvious that he would have no withdrawals, he was let go.

"Bud had stayed with Pastor Anderson and was more like the son he never had rather, than a guest in his home. The Pastor had gotten together several of the minister and deacons, and literally refurbished a new home in a much nicer neighborhood. On top of that, they furnished it as well.

"Mr. Paul was very grateful when he arrived, but Pastor Anderson was not through. He had hired him as janitor of the church. Bud was very happy to have a family. Both he and his father had been in terrible bondage, but there is nothing too hard for GOD!!!

"Bud moved back home and he and his father had a wonderful relationship. Pastor Anderson was just like a grandfather to Bud. They spent time together all of the time. What I did not know is that we would be classmates the upcoming year in school.

"As Fall approached, Nina and I had to get enrolled in school. I was excited. I had not been to school in America. At least not real school. I was always tutored from home. This was exciting for me.

"Mother was helping at the church that morning, and Father had always made it a point to take us and register us for school.

"Father and I had been fasting all week long. He said, 'The Lord wants to reveal something to you. Because this is where your ministry will be.'

"I trusted Father implicitly. He was a very consecrated man. Mother said he barely ate enough to keep a fly alive, but he always stayed in fellowship with God, so at a moment's notice, he could always get a prayer through. Father taught me to fast regularly to keep myself disciplined, because the flesh could easily rise up and cause problems.

"On the day Father, Nina and I went to register, I could see a huge dark cloud over the school. It looked pitch black, but there was not a cloud in the sky when we left home.

"Father said to me, 'Do you see your enemy?'

"'Yes,' I said.

"'What do you see written in it?'

"'Pleasure.'

"'Very good. That is what Satan is attempting to deceive these children with at this school. He has them constantly looking for pleasure, via drugs, illicit relationships of all kinds, or rebellion. Whatever makes them feel good at the time. Remember the vision when we first entered America. False pleasure was reporting to deception. Under this spirit they will do anything. But not you. You see and know.'

"We did not go into the school that day, but Father, Pastor Anderson, and I consecrated ourselves again unto the Lord. We met over Pastor Anderson's home the next day and he began to tell us of a coven that was on the outskirts of the city.

"He said that the Lord had revealed to him their plan for the schools in this area, and America as a whole. Every school year, they would take over the school board and force God out. No Bible no reference to Christ. Christmas was now called The Winter Holiday. And then they would go into the schools and talk to the children about what they called white witchcraft.

"There has been a dumbing down in America of how vile evil really is. Demons are portrayed as friends or guides. Vile lifestyles are depicted as normal, and witchcraft is shown as a source of help in time of trouble.

"But what is happening is that they get involved with witchcraft, and because they are not protected by the Blood of Christ, they have no defense when demons come to set up home in their bodies.

"'Now that you are here, we can take back what Satan has stolen through lies. They march around the building for three days straight 13 times. I and my congregation would fast and pray for the school and that kept it from totally taking over, but it was still there. The cloud looks darker than I have ever seen it before. Everything has a season, and it is time to kick Satan out of this area for good.'

"We went back to the school later that week and saw four females in very bright dresses. They were simply walking around the school. They did it 13 times, and then they left.

"We came back the next day at the same time and they came back the next day as well and did the same thing. They had one more time to do it and solidify the spirit of pleasure that was ruling this school.

"We three, Father, Pastor Anderson, and I, went back to the school for the third day, And we actually confronted the witches. It was about 12 midnight, in complete darkness. We stood there.

"Pastor Anderson said, 'Not this time.'

"The senior witch did not even look intimidated, but simply said, 'It is our hour.'

"Pastor Anderson replied, 'Your hour has now come to a close.'

"I felt the wind began to pick up. We all stood in the back of the school yard. The dark cloud above the school began to swirl and take shape. It was pitch black, with blood red eyes. It was huge, and had a silver sword in its hand.

"The witches began to chant in Latin. I understood exactly what they were saying. They were calling on the forces of darkness to destroy us and take possession of the school.

"I then saw Pastor Anderson take Father's hand, and Father took mine. He spoke the name of Jesus. His voice was thick, again with power. He bound false pleasure I saw the gold rope like bands come from heaven and bind him. I saw the witches fall to the ground and scream as if they were in pain.

"Then we were surrounded with black creatures with fangs claws and silver swords. We stood back-to-back. Father spoke the word of God, from the holy Bible.

"'No weapon formed against me will prosper—Isaiah 54:17—and I have authority to tread over serpents, snakes and scorpions and over all the power of the enemy and nothing shall by any means hurt me—Luke 10:19.' Just to name a couple.

"I saw the words take the shape of swords and literally sliced the creatures in half. They were bound with gold ropes, and sucked in to the large gaping whole above the school.

"The witches seemed to disappear. This school has been cleansed, but they had a sorority of witches in this school, and they will attempt to take this ground back.

"'Michael, it is your job to make sure that it does not happen on your watch.'

"'I understood my calling.'

"'They will be back, in a different form. But mark my words, they will be back.'

"Later that morning, Father brought Nina and I back to the school for registration.

"Nina never saw into the spirit realm much, but this time she did. The cloud was replaced with a glorious being standing over the school. He had golden sandals with a golden girdle. He had a huge gold sword that was drawn. His face was like lightning and his skin was bronze.

"Father asked her, 'Do you see?

"She said, 'Yes Father. I do and I understand.'

"Father produced our passports, citizenship papers, past school grades and current address. The young lady took the information and registered us for school.

"'Would both of you like to be in the same class?'

"'Yes,' Nina said, 'if possible.'

"She made out our schedules right there, and printed them out.

"'Feel free to walk around and find you classes. we will be open until 4:30 p.m. today'.

"Father, Nina, and I took her up on it. We walked around the school to find our classes. It was a very big facility with long wide halls. All of our classes were in the two main halls as the middle and high schools were combined down the hall from the principal's office.

"'Pretty easy to find,' Nina said.

"'Let's find the Gym,' I said. We began to follow the signs which lead us down in the building through a long descending hill like hall. When we got to the bottom, we could see a wonderful large gymnasium.

"Father said, 'This is a wonderful school from an appearance standpoint, but much prayer and fasting will have to be done to keep it free.'

"Nina and I both agreed, and we headed out of the back door for home.

"Nina had met a young lady at Mrs. Professors home, when her and mother visited, when we first arrived in this country.

"Her name was Anna. She was one of the church ladies' daughters who helped decorate our home. They hit it off right away, and she invited Nina over to a friend's house to play games, listen to music, etc.

"She invited me, but I chose to go with Father to see Pastor Anderson. Father would normally let me listen in on their conversations, because he always felt these things affected me as well as him.

"Pastor Anderson was a wonderful old man in age but not appearance. He barely looked older than Father, who was almost 41. We stepped in the parlor, and Pastor Anderson gave Father all of the details. Father explained why he wanted me to listen in on this, because he felt the Lord would call me to this church after he completed his ministrey.

"Pastor Anderson simply smiled and said, 'Yes. I know and I insist he listens in.'

"He took us into the parlor where he had already prepared lunch for both Father and I. Then I heard the most amazing story I had ever heard in my entire life."

Just then I heard, "Dinner."

Oh. not now, I thought.

Mr. Mike said, "Yes. I'm hungry. Aren't you?

Not really, I thought, but I did not want to offend him so I turned off my equipment and followed him into the dining room.

This was a wonderful, beautiful room. It was so polished and the table was impeccable. There was a curio, buffet, China cabinet, and an octagon dining table. It was absolutely beautiful. Everything was in its right place as usual.

I went to the lavatory to wash my hand and came back out ready to eat.

Mr. Mike said grace.

We had roasted chicken with broccoli, corn, corn bread spinach salad with almonds and mandarin oranges, cheese soup and Mrs. Dottie's famous tea.

I ate hurriedly because I was literally dying to hear Mr. Mike's awesome story. But Mrs. Dottie was not having that.

"Slow down," she said. "The story is older than you. It's not going anywhere. Tell me about your family?"

I really was not interested in my family, but it appeared they both were so I humored them.

"As you already know, I am from Perfect, California. A much different Perfect than when you visited so many years ago. There is prayer in school. The Bible is actually required reading. The courts have the Ten Commandments in them, and there are no denominations in the City. They are all simply called 'Cornerstone: The Church of the Lord Jesus Christ.' They all fellowship as one and there is absolutely no crime. When I go back home, we can still sleep with our doors open.

"I am the youngest of 4 boys. All of them became ministers, but me. From the crib, all I ever wanted to be is a writer. So I studied journalism through college. I was the editor of the paper, and class president through high school and College.

"So I was able to implement ideas and then write about them so the student body and faculty would support them. I had a wonderful time. After I graduated, I had an internship at the *New York Times* for two years. Then I landed my first real reporting job, where I am currently working."

"Why didn't you become a minister," Mrs. Dottie asked.

"Just not called, I guess. Father always told me that God gives you desires to be what he wants you to be, and all I have ever wanted to be was a journalist. So here I am. I have been waiting for a story like this one. I have been waiting for an opportunity like this one, where I could actually write my first book, and I think I have found it."

"How interesting," Mr. Mike said, as he took another sip of tea.

"The books that you have already written, Mr. Mike. I am an avid reader, but I can honestly say that I have never seen any of your work. They appear to be very interesting. Why haven't you published them yet?"

"I have been waiting on the Lord's timing, and it looks like that time has just about arrived."

We finished dinner, and Mr. Mike and I headed back to the study. I was pondering on what Mr. Mike had said. "That time is almost here."

What time, Mr. Mike?

He said, "Yes?"

"Time," I said.

He smiled and said, "Just keep listening. It will all become very clear to you."

Mr. Mike continued.

"Where was I? Oh yes. Father, Pastor Anderson, and I. We had just finished lunch at Pastor Andersons home when he, brought up my old Fathers name Mr. Ply. He said he is the one that has spearheaded the attack against the church in this area. He works within the political system. The judges, to be exact, to change various laws that this great country was founded on. He brings out the personal failures of all of the founding fathers and supports the alternate lifestyles in this area, using civil rights laws in an attempt to tear down the families. The reason the churches are so silent, is because he literally has deceived them.

"'Let's simply start from the beginning. The Lord revealed to me many years ago what the principality over America was. He also revealed that the regional warlock was right here in the town I was to living in. He is very wealthy and has literally taken the minds of most of the political leaders in this area when I came in more than 50 years ago.'

"'How,' Father asked.

"'He simply invites every new political leader or spiritual leader to his home. If they are not protected by the Blood of Christ, he has permission according to the spiritual laws to help them become possessed. Their minds are twisted and their thought so mingled with demonic activity, that all of their wrong doing appears in their own minds to be right. When I first arrived and took over this church, he tried that with me. I was invited through the mayor. Before I went to his home the Lord had already revealed Satan's plan to me so I had fasted, prayed, and was consecrated unto the Lord before I went. What he was not aware of, but I was, was that I could see into the spiritual realm to. I went because the Lord told me to go. Else, I would not have. The entire property was teaming with demonic activity, sent from the ruling principality to the regional warlock to dispense their masters bidding. One had been prepared to possess me. But it was not possible. I was already filled with The Holy Ghost and that with fire. When I entered the almost castle-like home, I could see beings. Red eyes looking at me. Mr. Ply stopped when he recognized who I was, and asked why I came. Even though he had invited me, the Lord had hid me from him so he could not see me. When I entered his home he felt and saw the presence of God on him. I told him I was sent there to let him know that this battle is already won and his master has already lost. He said that was what I thought, and he actually attempted to place a curse on me. I simply spoke the word, and in midair, I saw a sword of gold appear and slice through the spell of darkness he tried to send my way. Then two warrior demons, at least 7 feet tall, with black crow like wings appeared, and pulled solid silver swords from their sheathes. They had clawed feet, bodies like that of a bear, burning read eyes and the hatred that exhumed from them was literally nauseating. They took fighting posture as I spoke the word of God.'

"Then Pastor Anderson stopped telling his story and looked at me. 'Don't let anyone tell you the word of God is just a bunch of words put together by men. It is the power of God. It is JESUS CHRIST himself and when spoken by God's children in authority, it is powerful and very effective.'

"When he spoke the name, I could feel the power in it.

"Pastor Anderson continued, 'He said as I spoke, I said no weapon formed against me shall prosper. And I saw the demons' arms break off with their swords and hit the floor. I looked again and they had arms with no swords. They came at me and I spoke again. I could hear my voice it was absolutely thick with power. I said I have the power to tread on scorpions and over all of the work of the enemy and the large demons literally hit the floor as if someone was standing on it. Mr. Ply stood there in a trance. He suddenly came out of it and said I will destroy you. It is my time. I said your time is coming to an end and I walked out. I got into my car and left. As I traveled, I spoke to the Lord and said to him how long, Lord, before we take back this region for you? He said 40 years and he showed me you and your son, who used to be Mr. Ply's son. So that is why you are here. To take back the ground that lackadaisical Christians have given up. I have been in warfare for 40 plus years. Now fighting on every front.

"'Here, in America, we have a democracy. So the enemy attempts to take over the senate, congress, and courts on every level of government so that he can take over the next generation. I am the last pastor standing for Christ in this area. All others have been put to sleep. They unknowingly have witches and warlocks on their Deacon boards, Missionary Boards and even in their pulpits. They have been totally put to sleep, and witchcraft is prevalent in the churches in this area. They are more like social clubs. They have no power, and the word of God is never preached. The sermons are designed to make people feel good about being left in their sins on Sunday mornings. They no longer have Bible studies, or prayer services. The churches are in bondages, and Satan is continuing to wage warfare. The church has forgotten that there is a war going on, but with your recent arrival, they are now awakening.

"'For example, Pastor George, Pastor of the Greater Mount Zion Methodist Church, called me just last month. His daughter had been deathly ill, with Cancer of the brain, and they had given her up for death. His wife brought her to our Wednesday night Bible Service against her husband's advice but out of great desperation. The Lord miraculously healed her. The girl, when she came in was limp. Pail without color and barely breathing. Her mother brought her in a wheel chair. After prayer the young lady got out of the wheel chair and began to praise God for his mercy. Her appetite immediately returned. After service, she was being fed by a feeding tube. They took her to the hospital that night and had it removed. And I watched her eat a steak at the all-night diner myself. He called to give me his daughters report and she has absolutely no cancer in her body at all. Her doctor Dr. John Montgomery was a well-known and respected atheist in the community, wanted to meet with me to find out how I did it. I told him I did nothing. It was the God he did not believe in. I asked him would he like to meet him and he said yes. Because what I have seen is totally impossible. The girl was being eaten up with cancer one day, and the next day we cannot find a trace. There is more here than meets the eye. He accepted Christ that day and has been a faithful member of our church ever since. The father asked me why he could not pray her back to health. I told him the truth. He was a Ph.D. in Theology and Pastoral Studies but he did not know the God personally that he talked about.

"'So I introduced him. He has now been delivered from Satan and into the hand of God. He will be a great ally in our warfare. The Lord revealed to him that his senior Deacon was a warlock and had been placing spells on his congregation, including his daughter. So he had him removed and the church, is now receiving the pure word of God every Sunday, and they now have Wednesday night prayer meetings, which they had stopped for lack of participation.

"'Pastor Shimmy, of the African American Episcopal Church, recently called to tell me that he had seen me in a vision, preaching the gospel to him and had a great urgency to call me. I told him that one night while sleeping, I dreamt I was speaking with him and I was warning him because he was in the process of being deceived, and one of his associate ministers was actually a warlock sent by Satan too keep the church asleep. He said I had explained to him that the only way out was JESUS. He said he prayed the sinner's prayer immediately when he woke up. And was immediately born again.

"'He had a ministers meeting with all of his associate ministers and had them all profess their faith in the fact that Jesus had come in the flesh to suffer and die for humanity. He told them only by the spirit of God can a person make this declaration if they cannot then you are not GOD's. His associate pastor who was actually his assistant pastor began to have convulsions right there, his convulsions were so serious that he literally began to throw up blood. They did call the hospital and he is still in a comma to this day. Their church has broken out in a revival, and they still go see that assistant pastor daily and pray for his salvation and soul.

"'Pastor Bogey from Trinity Lutheran just called today, to thank me for coming out to the hospital when he was given only 6 months to live with prostate cancer. I and my assistant pastors laid hands on him and believed God for his total and complete healing. He wanted to tell me that the doctors could find no trace of cancer in his body today. And the list goes on. there are over 200 churches in this area, of every denomination imaginable, and 123 have had pretty recent conversion to the true Christ within the last six and half months. So when the professor came to my church, the Lord told me that he would know the man who would take my place. When he told me your name and described you to me, I knew you were the one to knock the regional warlock off of his throne and take back California and America for the Lord. Your training is not only theology but law. Correct?'

"I did not know that Father had studied law and had a license to practice in Sweden, he never shared that with me. He understood law just as much as he understood theology. I always knew my father was remarkable, but now I knew just how remarkable. Pastor Anderson said we have much work to do. I have noticed a pattern, which on every Halloween the Church loses more ground, the people in America look at it as a kids' holiday and do not understand the powerful effect it has on our children. A lot of children in this area are un-churched and definitely not Christian. Every Halloween they get involved in all types of cultic activities, Ouija boards, haunted houses, seances, Tara cards, witchcraft, horoscopes and psychic readings. They watch all night horror films which fill them with fear, and you know and I know fear acts just like faith in reverse. It is how the enemy gets a choke hold on them in an attempt to destroy them.

"This is all done in the name of fun. These things lead to demon possession, and they do not even realize why they are becoming more and more rebellious, angry and perverted. There is a place here called The Willow. Children come from miles around to visit the haunted homes in that area. It has almost become a landmark. I have seen it. It is filled with demons, clamoring to possess and destroys yet another child.

"The children who have no covering simply come out possessed, and it gets worse every single year. Children are being deceived continually and destroyed, and no one has an answer except for the true church of Jesus Christ.

"Your son will help us tremendously in this area, he will help lead the youth out of this bondage. I have seen it. This Halloween will be different, and I have been waiting for this for a long time. We must concentrate ourselves. This Halloween we will actually take back all of the ground that we have lost in the past 50 years. In the past, even churches would participate by placing skeletons on their doors with jack lanterns in their yards.

"But not this year. They had called A meeting with the recently converted 123 pastors in the area. He was actually mobilizing the Body of Christ. And he wanted Father to be there, so that he could be introduced as the new pastor and take the lead in this warfare when Pastor Anderson was called home.

"This is when Pastor Anderson began to do something that had not been done since the church was birthed into the Earth. He broke down denominational lines. There was no Catholic, Methodist, Baptist, Lutheran, Church of God, or Church of Christ. Even the Jehovah's Witnesses and the Mormons in the area converted to the true Bible. It was all about the person of JESUS. All differences were set aside so that God, and God alone, would get the glory. The church was becoming one.

"Pastor Anderson continued, 'I do not have much time. The Lord has said my work is almost complete, and I am soon to go home.'

"Father and I had witnessed the war in the heavenly when the denominational barriers were being broken down, and they came into true fellowship with the most high God himself, through his wonderful Son.

"Both of us at night when we would sleep would see the victories in our dreams. We could see massive angels of God and of Satan combating in midair. There was nothing between them.

"The heavenly angels were taking ground. No one got tired. The evil angels simply began to lose more and more ground.

"The evil angels had a shadowy form with blood red eyes, and huge bat like wings with silver swords. The majestic angels were bronze in color with huge white wings trimmed in gold with gold swords.

"Every time a minister was delivered, this warfare went on in the heavens.

"Pastor Anderson said to father that he should expect an invitation in the mail for dinner to Mr. Ply's home shortly after his death.

"'He is losing much ground, and his master will require an answer. He will have an idea that it is you.

"Father said, 'Yes. I will be prepared.'

"Father got extreme joy out of doing the work of the Lord. It gave him great pleasure.

"We left that evening. Father shared some of what Pastor Anderson had to say with Mother and Nina. As was our custom whenever there was a spiritual revelation, the whole family would come together in prayer to keep father strong in his warfare. But this was a new country, and Nina and I had no idea we were about to enter into warfare as well."

"It's that time," Mrs. Dottie said.

It was almost midnight.

How time flew!

Zahede had come to pick me up, but had gotten into conversation with Mrs. Dottie, and she had lost track of time.

I apologized again for keeping Mr. Mike up past his appropriate time of rest.

I gathered my things and said 8:00 a.m. tomorrow, that will be fine.

"I think we will be able to wrap up soon."

I smiled and said, "I hope not."

He smiled and said, "Good night."

Zahede never interrupted when he arrived. He just sat and waited.

He enjoyed being at Mr. Mike's home. He said it was so peaceful, he could stay there all day. He would simply come and sit in the rocking chair on the porch and begin having conversation with Mrs. Dottie about his boys, he would never come in and interrupt.

As we traveled back to the city, I asked Zahede, "Why have you not interviewed Mr. Mike?"

"Oh, I have his story has been printed in many newspapers around the world, because of his advanced age. He said he always knew who would write a book of his life and when he met him it would be written. I guess that person must be you. What a wonderful opportunity you have been afforded."

I smiled and said, "How did you know I was writing a book?"

"Do you know how many reporters I have been asked to bring out here? Hundreds. Their interviews last all of one to two hours, but you have been coming back for more than a week in a half. You must be the one."

"Interesting," I thought to myself as we traveled. "What a wonderful land this is."

"Yes," Zahede said, "it is indeed."

When I arrived at the hotel, there was a message for me to call the office. So when I got back to my room, I called my boss.

He wanted to know how it was going and how long before I would be returning.

I said, "At least another couple of days. But it will be worth every dollar we are spending on my stay."

My editor had known something I was not aware of. Every editor in every major newspaper had wanted to publish Mr. Mike's full story because of his advanced age, and not only that he had documented influence over every political leader from around the world for more than 50 years.

He had hoped I would be the one, because he knew we once lived in the same small town, he hoped there would be a connection. He had himself attempted to get the interview just 15 years ago, but he was unsuccessful.

"Take as longs as you need. And get plenty of photos."

"I have," I said goodbye, hung up the phone, and went to bed.

I thought as I drifted off to sleep. What a wonderful land to be in, and what a magnificent life. How could a world so real not be seen by so many, including me?

I drifted off to sleep, thanking God for this great opportunity.

The next morning, I pounced out of bed. Showered, shaved, brushed, and was down stairs again too early. So I went into the restaurant for a little breakfast, before I headed out.

The Manager came and asked to sit with me for a moment.

"Yes of course," I said.

"Learning anything from Mr. Mike?"

"I have learned enough in these few days to write 100 books," I said laughingly.

"Yes. I look forward to reading it myself. Mr. Mike had always said that there is only one person he would allow to write his story. Hundreds have tried. I know, because they have all stayed right here. They are normally gone within about four or five days, with the interview itself lasting mabey a couple of hours. But you. You must be the one."

How interesting that everyone would know that I was going to write a book on Mr. Mike, when I just figured it out myself a couple of days ago.

Zahede came to my table and said, "Are you ready?"

As always, I said, "Yes."

"Let's go."

When we arrived, I always enjoyed walking through the little white picket fence and watching the hundreds off tiny pastel butterflies fly around he flowers. I was greeted warmly by Mrs. Dottie and lead to Mr. Mike study. He was waiting for me this morning, with that same wonderful carefree smile.

"Good morning. Are you ready to continue?"

"Yes, yes!!"

"Then let's begin.

"I was anxious about attending the meeting with the 123 pastors, but Father said I would not be going to that.

"'But why,' I asked Father.

"'Because you need to focus on the battle ground you have been given.'

"'The school?'

"'Yes,' Father said. 'School begins in two weeks and you need to be prepared.'

"From that moment on, Father and I would rise at five every morning and pray for one hour. We would study our scriptures for one hour, and we would fast breakfast every day for the next two weeks. When school began, guess who was in our class?"

I did not have a clue, and asked, "Who?"

"Bud," he said with a smile. "Bud was in all of our classes. Coincidence? Not hardly. Bud had been a trouble maker for most of his life, after the death of his mother, and his father becoming the town addict. He felt no need to try. He just went to school to get away from his father. His reputation had proceeded him. People moved out of his way as he walked in the room Bud was 13 and already stood 6 feet tall and about 230lbs of muscle, but now he was clean as far as the school was concerned, still a trouble maker."

Chapter 5

"When I first saw him, I could not tell where the dirt stopped and the person began. But he was doing well now.

"I had seen him many times at church, but for some reason, we never really talked about school.   But there he was big as day and walked right over and sat by me and spoke.

"'Hiya, PK!'

"That is what he always called me. That stands for Preachers Kid.

"Bud was very smart and literally got A's in all of his classes. He said school was always easy for him, but he never had a reason to try after his mother passed away. His father never seemed to care, so he just got by, but now because of Jesus, he had purpose.

"He said, 'I am going to be a preacher, just like Pastor Anderson, when I grow up.'

"'Good for you,' I used to tease. 'As big as you are, you will probably scare people into the Kingdom.'

"Every class I was in was noticeably quiet. No disruptive behavior.

"Apparently in the past, Bud was the cause of most of it. Anyone that attempted to steal his thunder, he literally put through a wall. So no one said much around Bud for the first few months of school. When they saw, and really believed, that he had changed, classes livened up a little.

"We found out he was even known at the high school, and special arrangements were being made in anticipation of him coming. He had been known for putting students and teachers through walls.

"However, one day when the kids began to hang out in the hall and the windows, and would not listen to the teachers, Bud stood up and said as big as day, 'I can still beat anybody down that gets in my way, but I really don't want to have to.'

"It had gotten out that Bud was a holy roller. And some of the gangs in the school thought that meant he was soft, so they would challenge him. The gangs were not as violent as they used to be normally. There would be guns. But because of the spiritual warfare had taken the school back, it was mostly just threats.

"Guns never seemed to make it through the door anymore. Bud had absolutely no fear regardless. He would say out loud, 'try me!'

"So one day a kid (He was in middle school but a high school gang), did and said, 'What will a Bible thumper like you do to me?'

"Bud said, 'After school. Myers Park. Be there, and we will see.'

"When the word got out that there would be a fight every student at the school was there.

"Bud said, 'Now. We can fight and I can beat you down. Or you can simply shut up in class, so I can learn, and you can save face.'

"He whispered this in his ear, and told me later.

"But the boy had brought a knife from home, pulled it, and said, 'Let's see.'

"Bud again showed no fear, and somehow, I am not sure to this day how he got the knife from that kid, but he did he, broke it, and said, 'Next.'

"It scared the kid so bad that he and his whole gang ran. We talked later. He said that the Lord had already showed him what to do. He simply did it and got the victory.

"'You cannot go wrong with the Lord,' he would always say.

"I agreed, and we all walked home together.

"Anna caught up with us and asked us to walk her home. She lived only one block over from where we lived. Nina had said that she had noticed how nervous she seemed to be the last couple of days. She would not tell her why. Bud said he could not walk her home, because he had to help his dad at the church before dinner, and Nina had to help Mother with dinner. So that just left me.

"'I will walk you home. See you guys later,' I said. 'How have you been doing, Anna? You seem to be crying all of the time lately.'

"She simply sniffed and said it is nothing. When we got to her house, she asked if I could come in. I said for only a minute. It was then that I caught it out of the side of my eye. That same disgusting spirit of Lust that was in our home was now in Anna's home. But how could I cast it out here without being noticed. I asked Anna where the bathroom was and went.

"I had been consecrated unto God. I knew where my authority came from. I remembered my training and, more importantly, the word of God. I turned on the water, and spoke out of my spirit. The thing came into the bathroom with me.

"The smell was horrible. The maggots looked bigger and nastier than the one in our home.

"It spoke first and said, 'This is my home.'

"I remembered my training, and spoke only the word of God. 'Wherever my feet tread, the Lord has given that land to me and I am here now and I bind you spirit of Lust and command you in the name of Jesus never to come back into this home again!'

"When I spoke the name, my voice always sounded thick with power when I spoke it in warfare.

"I saw the golden bands take hold of it, and I saw a large dark hole appear in the ceiling, and it was sucked in. I flushed the toilet and found Anna.

"I asked Anna's mom, Mrs. Pillard, a very quiet woman with a very quiet voice. 'Is their any inappropriate material in the home?'

"'How did you know?'

"'The Lord has revealed it to me.'

"'I am ashamed to say it for the last two months, my husband has been hording it on the internet and in magazines. They are in his study.'

"I said to her, 'Mrs. Pillard. I know you believe God, because you attend Pastor Anderson's church. Your husband was bound because of these articles in your home. The thing has been cast out, but we must get rid of all of this filth.'

"To this day, I do not know why she would listen to a little boy, but she did. It was at that time that Mr. Pillard walked in the door sobbing uncontrollably. He said on his way home from work when he was stopped at a stop light that the spirit of God convicted him of his sin and told him to throw all of it away now.

"'I must do it now. Will you help me, Michael?'

"'Yes,' I said.

"He had tons of it. I could not look upon it the words, and the pictures seemed to be blurred as I picked them up and put them in trash sacks. A total of two garbage bags full of inappropriate material. He apologized to his wife and daughter for what he had allowed in his home, and said that with the Lords help, it will never happen again.

"We took both sacks, and put them in Mr. Pillards truck. He then went in and wiped his entire computer clean, and put a blocker on in so that pop-ups would not come up again. That is how he got started. He used his computer frequently to do research for his job. Some inappropriate material popped up and he began to explore them and the different websites they led to.

"He said before he knew it, he would be up in the middle of the night reviewing what he should not have been reviewing. Buying things he should not have been buying. It just snowballed and he said he could not help himself. He said he felt driven. He then apologized with me in the room to his wife and daughter. whom he had become extremely abusive to. He said, 'I am sorry.'

"But all of that is gone now. I left their home about one and half hours later, and I was almost late for dinner. I ran in to tell Father of our victory. He was excited I was operating in the ministry that the Lord had for me. He then told me that he was going to run for school board council.

"Great, I thought. Father was very intelligent, and I knew he would be an asset anywhere he was. He had a parent bring a school book to him one day, while he was working with Pastor Anderson. It was a book of incantations. In short, how to be a white witch.

"'White witches are not bad,' the teacher told the parent. 'The children are simply reading the book to get an understanding of other religions in other countries, since America is a Christian nation.'

"The mother was extremely upset. It was a mandatory read for an English project, discussing the religions in different countries. This book had incantations and spells practiced in England for hundreds of years.

"Pastor Anderson then sat Father, Nina, and I down, and elaborated on a subject that he had broached when we first came to this city.

"'In this country, evil has disguised itself as good. Demons come in pleasing shapes, pretending to care for people and wanting to help them. There is a huge coven, right on the outskirts of town and they recruit young children to be warlocks and witches. White witch or black witch, all are evil and desire to deceive all who come in contact with it.

"'Halloween is their holiday. These celebrations take them deeper and deeper into the caravans of darkness. They are taught spells on how to be popular, pretty, and smart. Demons disguise themselves as guides, and take control of them. They try to get them to believe that they are good spirits or passed on relatives who only want to help them find their true potential.

"'After a while they are so taken over, that the evil they do, they believe is good. So young people your ages begin to delve into Ouija boards, Tarot cards, burning sage, placing curses on each other, etc.

"The demons give them what they are looking for, so they can gain more control of that person. So much so, that the person is not even aware of who they are. They eventually kill themselves, become outcast or they are placed into an insane asylum, away from people so they do not hurt themselves or anyone else.

"That is why the insane asylum in this community has had a 40 percent growth rate among teens in the last 25 years. The occult is rampant in this country, and so-called Christian parents are allowing their own children to watch cartoons, movies, play with games, and they do not even realize that Satan is attached to them, looking for a way to possess or oppress them, and steal their children's childhood from them. They are so successful that a lot of children feel that this is just the way they are.

"'It is very sad. Which is why I hope Mr. Finn will accept the offer of running for the school board. To help get rid of some of this demonic influence. It will take much prayer, but we will succeed if you accept.'

"Father smiled and said, 'Of course I will.'

"The fight for the board seat was fierce. There was a board of nine members. Two atheists, one agnostic, three realists that simply stayed politically correct, and three witches. This battle would have to be won in the heavens.

"Father campaigned, but was fought against as being a bigot who hated anyone that was different. The Christian faith was totally attacked as being bigoted, because of their stand on sexual immorality, abortion, violence, etc.

"The Bible is very black and white in these areas and Satan hates it. The Church came to the forefront and began to pray and fast.

"God said, 'If my people who are called by my name would humble themselves and pray, and seek my face turn from their wicked ways, then will I hear from heaven and heal their land.' (2 Chronacles 7:14).

"All of the churches in the community began to call on the Lord for help. Father ran on the platform of if the Bible cannot be in the schools, then neither can witchcraft.

"This angered Mr. Ply to no end. You see, Satan's biggest weapon is that no one believes he is orchestrating all of this human confusion. But he is. I remembered when I lived in America long ago how my old father. Mr. Ply would chant in the night, I would watch him and I could literally see him leave his body. The next day, without fail, when Father would allow me to watch TV, there would be some terrible disaster with the youth.

"He would normally do it on Friday and Saturday nights, when we would watch the news. He would always point out how he influenced this death or placed illness on someone or caused some type of destruction. He was always about his master's business.

"If the church would have been as diligent in America, it would not be in the condition it is in now. I was so glad I was on the winning side, and I too would help present the true God to the teens of the area.

"The Battle went on for three solid weeks, of all types of negative media coverage against Father and his faith. On the night of the final vote, Father had anointed the entire Board of Education office with holy oil.

"Mr. Ply was supposed to be there for the vote. All of the lead community officials voted, and it was believed that Mr. Ply's vote would sway the remainder of the people. But he never showed up, and Father won by a land slide."

Even though it was unethical for a person giving their life story to be interrupted, I had to ask, "I'm sorry why didn't he show up?"

Mr. Mike said, "Father had held him at bay. He could not get across the anointed oil of God, and he had tried, desperately. I had snuck downstairs to see what would happen, because I knew there would be a serious battle. I saw Mr. Ply as he got out of his car and made his way across the street he walked into an invisible wall. He fell down and got back up and hit it again. He stood back and began to conjure. I saw a very large entity appear and attempt to hit the building with his sword, but it bounced off of the invisible barrier and broke. He walked all around the building and the same thing happened over and over again. He left in a fit of rage, and Father was voted the newest School of Education Board Member unanimously.

"The witches were confounded, and voted for Father. It was a true miracle, because he should not have won, but if God says yes.

"He worked very hard and succeeded in getting all types of foul literature out of the school systems. The school eventually became the best in the entire country, and still is the last time I checked. And is The Bible still mandatory reading?"

"Yes, it is," I replied.

"That is wonderful! One Saturday, Father took me to the outskirts of the town. It was filthy and littered with drugs, needles, papers, people my age, and a little older. It was full of teenagers. There was perversion of every kind in the streets, and there were bars, inappropriate clubs, and inappropriate literature shops throughout the area.

"He would say, 'Look around. This is where the kids you go to school with come on Friday and Saturday night in search of love through pleasure.'

"It was called the Willow, and all of the kids that talked about this place were always experimenting with the occult. They thought it was harmless and practiced regularly. Some looked the part. Pentagram necklaces, black lip stick, all black clothing etc. But not all. Some fancied themselves white witches and remained clean in their appearance, but within they were full of darkness and had made up their own morality. They were simply deceived. They wanted real power and their parents by living lazy Christian lives had not shown them the true power of God. They wanted, the kind of power that the dark side was more than willing to show them for their souls.

"The demons would come in slowly, and begin to place their minds in bondage, cause, killings, gang activities, destruction, and the list goes on.

"We would walk around and place religious tracs that we had prayed over, anointed and placed them in different establishments bathrooms, on their counters anywhere the Lord would have us place them. The tracs we would give out were entitled 'Do You want Real Power???? Look inside.'

"Our church address was on the back and invited them to come to our church the next day. Satan had claimed this area, but father would always say, 'The earth is the Lords and the fullness thereof the world and they that dwell therein.' (Psalms 24:1).

"Father would go wherever he was sent, and the Lord had told him to begin to come here every Saturday night with me. After about a month of doing this, I noticed that people with black makeup, half drunk, high, or both, were starting to come in.

"Pastor Anderson and Father had already instructed the ushers what to do when they recognized these individuals. They had a special place right up front. As time went on more and more began to come in. So Pastor Anderson said it was time to build a larger sanctuary. Pastor Anderson was a very skillful man of finance.

"Now. Do you remember the 123 pastors I was talking about?"

"Yes," I said.

"Well, all of these young and old men were literally on fire for the Lord. The reason The Willow was running over with youth and the insane asylum had grown 40 percent in the last 25 years is because the pastors were out of place. God was on the move through Pastor Anderson. He had called them all together to put them back in place. I was present when he introduced my Father as the Pastor elect of his current church.

"All were sad to see Pastor Anderson go, and so they all asked where he was going.

"'To Heaven,' he said with a smile. 'I have almost finished my work, and Pastor Finn will be taking my place and leading the battle for the soul of this community and country.'

"The church in Perfect was just like the church out of the New Testament. Pastor Anderson had completely laid out what area of the community each church should take, according to the Lord's leading. Two were in charge of the The Willow with with Father and me. Others were assigned bars, clubs, abortion clinics, schools, courts, city council, media, paper, radio, TV…the list went on.

"The church was starting to realize that we were in a real battle. As he called them out, he would ask, 'Is this what the Lord has shown you?'

"They always replied, 'Yes.'

"The battle was definitely afoot. The church was doing real spiritual battle for the first time in this area of the world. Each church fasted, prayed, praised and took the whole armor of the Lord to do battle with Satan daily. But Satan was not going to give up easily.

"Pastor Anderson worked very hard to get the building expanded, because even though he had about 50 acres that the church owned, the parking was overwhelming the neighborhood, and the city council, which was being controlled by Mr. Ply, attempted to ban church one Sunday, because of the number of cars.

"So 10 acres was sectioned off for parking alone. The other 40 acres increased the sanctuary size to hold 3,000 people, plus a school. This would be one of the biggest structures in the city, and Mr. Ply would fight it with everything he had. The church would be almost as big as community college in terms of land."

I interrupted again and said, "That is where I got my degree from, and my brother currently pastors the largest church in Perfect. I'm sorry. I didn't mean to interrupt."

Mr. Mike simply smiled and said, "Now you are beginning to understand. Stay with me though.

"Once the sanctuary was complete and dedicated in just four short months. Pastor Anderson called for now 200 churches that had, had true conversions to say goodbye. Father now pastored the largest church in the community, and he was the newest one in town. One day, Pastor Anderson came by to say goodbye. He hugged me and looked up and told father, 'Train him well. Michael is a powerful name for a powerful warrior for the Lord.'

"He left, went home that night, and never woke up.

"We found out later, when Father went over the next day, when he was late for his appointment at the church. He had asked Father to meet him there. Father did not know what for. He normally would tell him, but he did not.

"Everything was wrapped up when Pastor Anderson died, so father stepped into the position with great ease. When he was funeralized, there were so many people that the 3,000 seated church would not contain them all.

"He was laid to rest right there on the property in the church graveyard, next to his wife. As Pastor Anderson had said, Father was invited to Mr. Ply's home for dinner immediately after his death.

"He was more than aware of what was happening. He had hoped to destroy Father and take over his mind, as he had the others, because something had happened. The hold Satan had held on 200 pastors had been broken in a matter of about 9 short months. He was losing his control that he had held for decades, and he knew Pastor Anderson was the cause of it. He had to destroy his successor.

"'Then why go,' I asked Father.

"'It is the Lords will. The Lord has hidden me well. The enemy has not been able to see me. He just knows he is being defeated and he is trying to find out how and by whom."

Mr. Mike continued and said, "I wanted to see what would happen. So, on the evening that Father was invited to have dinner, I snuck up the mountain to see. I felt an old fear as I began to travel up the mountain on my motorbike. I had consecrated myself to the Lord, so I had no fear of demons, but this place had held very bad memories for me. Of loneliness, confusion, pain...the list went on. it was about a nine mile trek from the bottom to the top of the mountain. It was on a Saturday. So I had plenty of time and light.

"When I got there, I knew exactly where they would be having dinner. In the old dining hall where my old father would have them oppressed in their spirits. He would invite them in, and when he saw their lack of power, they were simply taken over. But not Father.

"My dad was covered by the Blood of Christ himself. Satan could not penetrate that armor.

"I was not invited, but youthful curiosity got the better of me. I had to see for myself. So I climbed up the side of the home, and sat on the ledge. Even though it was white in color, it felt dark. The stones were pristinely clean but they still felt draining. This property had been dedicated to Satan, and I knew it.

"I sat on a ledge, about four feet wide and five feet across. I could look right into the dining hall. Just as I took my spot, my old father, Mr. Ply, and my real Father walked into the room. My old father walked to the end of the 20-foot table, and then jerked.

"He turned suddenly and said, 'You will not win this battle.'

"Father said, 'It is already won.'

"Mr. Ply was unable to pick up on who my father was in the Lord until that very moment. I found out later that The Lord is able to hide his people so Satan cannot find or see them.

"Father had been well hid. That is when I realized that God really does have all power, and Satan is only a created being, and not a creator. So God was totally in control. I felt safety for my Father from that point on.

"I heard Mr. Ply say, 'So you are the cause of the ground being lost. We will get it back. We control the political system, media, TV, newspapers, movies, toys, games. Your Christian parents put their children to sleep at night with demons, totally unaware of our scheme.

"You see," Mr. Mike said, "God said, 'While looking me straight in my eyes My people perish for a lack of knowledge.' (Hosea 4:6). You see what would happen," Mr. Mike elaborated, "is all toys that were remotely associated with the occult, either by looks or power, were brought to the regional warlock in that area before it went to the stores. They were prayed over and dedicated to Satan, causing familiar spirits to be attached to them. So children were being influenced. If the parents were not real Christians with the power of discernment. You see, real Christian parents' children are sanctified by their believing parents. Satan cannot get in to possess, but he can oppress and unprotected children are fair game. Their behavior changes drastically, and they are then taken over by an ancient evil whose desire is to destroy them by whatever means necessary.

"I had seen Mr. Ply conger over toys, clothing items, cards, etc. etc. and I could see the spirit lay hold of the items. The trucks were literally brought directly to our home. He had very powerful contacts, and all regional warlocks work together to control such things. This happened all of the time. I was being trained to do the same thing, so I could be prepared when I took my place as the regional warlock.

"Mr. Ply continued, 'Have you not noticed our handy work? Have you not seen the movies coming out of Hollywood? Have you not seen the increase of cultic activity? The total acceptance of perversion? Even though we have lost some ground with you here, we will get it back and rule the world.'

"Father then said softly to him, 'Mr. Ply. The Lord has revealed to me that you do not have much time on this earth.'

"Mr. Ply screeched, 'That is not true! I have lived for one hundred years in this Earth, and I will live longer than you!'

"Father said, 'You have been deceived, and the battle is already won. God is waiting for you to make your decision for him.'

"'I have my forces ready to take you down,' said Mr. Ply. 'What has your God done for me? He left me sick, homeless and penniless.'

"'And that is how Satan has presented Him to you. Satan is a liar.'

"You see, Mr. Ply came from extremely humble beginnings, and was born with polio and placed in an orphanage within a small village where he was starved, neglected, and abused, while being teased unmercifully as he grew up by his peers.

"A witchdoctor cured him and dedicated him to Satan as a child. Mr. Ply thought the way to repay such a favor was to give his life to the darkness. His goal would be to serve his master with everything in him. He thought Satan loved him because he had healed his body. The witchdoctor adopted him, raised him in witchcraft, and once he passed, he became the witchdoctor for the village. Not realizing that Satan was a deceiver.

"Father simply repeated himself, 'You do not have long upon the Earth, and if you die in this condition you will surly go to Hell.'

"'To rule!' Mr. Ply exclaimed.

"'To suffer for all of eternity,' Father said. 'Even Satan does not rule Hell. He will suffer for all of eternity with you.'

"'I have real power now,' and he waved his hand, and the room was full of demons all around Father. Small, large, hissing, and spitting, cursing and slithering. Some looked like snakes, some dogs other combinations of animals. Half bat and bear, half buzzard and snake. They were horrible looking.

"But father did not flinch.

"'I have come to tell you that your time is ending. There is still forgiveness if you chose it but it has to be your choice.'

"I thought it was too late for Mr. Ply, because of his total acceptance of Satan, but he was deceived as a boy. Therefore, still giving an opportunity by a loving God to miss Hell.

"Mr. Ply looked down. Then looked up.

"'Never!' He exclaimed. He pulled his hands back and fire came from both of them.

"Father did not move. A shield of blue gold light protected him.

"'No weapon formed against me can prosper,' Father said.

"I looked around, and then I saw the most magnificent display of power I had ever seen. Even greater than in Africa. There were angels. Huge and very muscular with long white garments. They had gold sashes with gold swords and shields. They were holding back all of the demons in the room. Their faces were like lightning and the demons hissed, as if in pain from the light.

"Father then turned and walked out of the room. Mr. Ply dropped to his knees, as if his strength had been drained from him. Father walked out of the house.

"I jumped down and began to ride my bike back to the city. I tried to get back home, before Father new I was gone. My bike would not get me there fast enough, but I tried.

"When I finally did get home. I tried to sneak into the house. Father heard me and simply said, 'Did you learn anything?'

"'Yes,' I said. 'The word of God is truly a weapon that can be used rather there is one or 1000 demons, greater is he that is in us than he that is the world (1 John 4:4). The Bible is real.'

"'You have learned a valuable powerful lesson, but never ever go into an environment like that unless the Lord himself has called you. That could have been very dangerous for you if the Lord had not protected and hid you.'

"'Yes Father, I said, and went to my room.

"That night as I slept. I had the most unusual dream. I dreamt I was at the mental hospital, and I could see these things in black cloaks stabbing at the patience with jagged swords. Some were on top of their heads, stabbing them in their brains. Others were being stabbed in the face. Some in the back of the head. It was terrible.

"The things seemed to derive great joy from this as they laughed uncontrollably.

"I asked, 'Lord what does this mean?'

"'This is a big part of your ministry,' the Lord said to me. 'These people are being tormented by demons that they unknowingly invited into their own lives by witchcraft. The medication that is given to them simply opens them up even more so.

"'There is a girl here by the name of Sarah Cummings. She has a great call on her life. She was experimenting with witchcraft, and because of it, lost her mind. She was given a ring when she joined what she thought was a sorority, but in truth, it was a coven. It caused her to become very loose with her morals, reckless, and paranoid. When her parents told her she could no longer participate in the group and tried to take the ring off her finger, she pulled a knife and almost cut her father's hand off. It was because of this she was sent here. I have sent you to restore her.'

"I could see Sara. She was strapped down by her wrist, ankles, thighs, and her chest her hair was wet and matted, The Lord instructed me to look up, and I looked up, and I could see what she had gone through earlier that day. There were four creatures around her, stabbing her in her head, telling her she was going to go to Hell today. it wouldn't be long now. Sara was hitting her head up against a padded wall. So the attendants came in a placed a straightjacket on her, and left her in the padded floor. The things came back and continued to stab her in the head, and tell her she was going to Hell today.

"She was slobbering and crying as she began to hit her head against the floor.

"I said, 'Lord her eyes are so empty. Where is she?'

"The Lord said, 'Look again.'

"I could see Sara in a jail cell, in a dingy room. She was up to her waste in what looked like huge leeches and waste. She had fallen into them when she grabbed the bar over the room, and lifted herself up. The leeches had consumed the lower part of her body. As she pulled herself up, her body would reappear. But just then the bar would disappear and she would fall back in the pit to be consumed again."

"How horrible," I said.

"Yes. She started like most kids. She just wanted to be popular. She began to spend more and more time at The Willow. She could no longer control her own thoughts. Thoughts of suicide and murder plagued her day and night. Her sisters in the coven had dedicated her as a sacrifice so they could become more popular, and have more things, more money.

"Sara was slowly losing her mind. It was being taken over by this ancient evil, whose desire was to destroy her and all humans. The group that she was with think they are controlling her, but when Satan is finished with using them as recruits, he will destroy them as well.

"Her family could not control her, so they had her committed. She stopped eating, painted her room black, surrounded herself with crystals, and began to call on good spirits for help, but they were only demons in disguise. After a while, all she would do is spit and curse. They have cleansed her body of the drugs she dabbled in as well, but the spirits she picked up on her journey are relentless and will not give up until she is dead and her soul in Hell.

"You see, she is in an unregenerate state and if she dies like this she will go to Hell because she chose wrongly. Her father and mother are new believers, and pray for her every second of every day. I could see their faces. Yes, they have just joined our church.

"I did not know they had another daughter. I only saw the one. The Lord said I have sent you to deliver her. I was suddenly back in the room standing over Sara. I called her name Sara, in the name of Jesus Christ I rebuke and bind every demon that has bound you and I call your mind whole.

"I said, 'Sara do you renounce Satan and the control he has over you?'

"She chokingly said, 'Yes. Help me, please.'

"I saw shadows leaping off of her as if they were leaping off of a hot stove. They screamed as they left, and there was no confrontation. They simply left her. At once Sara looked up at me and smiled.

"I immediately woke up. It was day.

"I hurried and got dressed and told Father what had happened. He called the Cummings to let them know that they should go see Sara this morning. The Lord has delivered her. Apparently, Father had been praying with the family about their daughter.

"Father called me from the Church later that evening when I had gotten home, and said, 'Your willingness to yield to God has given this family back their daughter. We went to see her today and lead her in the sinner's prayer. The doctors have given her a clean bill of health. She is coherent and smiling. We gave her a Bible to read. She is feeding herself, and has passed every exam they have thrown at her today. They just want to watch her for a couple of days, but she could be in church by this Sunday.'

"Then Father said, 'All praise to our Lord and Savior Jesus Christ. He is worthy.'

"I agreed, 'He is more than worthy.'

I hung up the phone, and went back to my room to finish my homework. I looked forward to possibly meeting Sara on Sunday.

"That Sunday, Sara did indeed come to church and father had the family sit up front so that he could give Sara a moment to tell her testimony.

"We had never met, but just then she looked over at me and mouthed, 'Thank you.'

"She remembered me from a dream she had.

"The Lord does work in mysterious ways. She gave all the praise unto the Lord and came over immediately to thank me for being obedient to God.

"'It is your faithfulness to him why I am standing here today. Thank you,' she said, 'thank you and thank you.'

"She hugged my neck and began to cry. 'Thank you. Thank you.'

"'You are welcomed in the Lord,' was my reply. She let me go, turned her head and left with her family.

"I saw Sara many times in school, ministering to kids that were experimenting with drugs and witchcraft. She would tell her testimony and how bad it was. She had absolutely no fear of telling her testimony, even though she was told on several occasions that religion was not allowed in school, because there was a separation of church and state.

"She would always say, 'I am not talking about religion but a person. The son of God, Jesus, who is the Christ. The one who saved my mind, just look at me and know that he is alive and well.'

"One of the counselors became very angry with Sara and threatened to take her from her parents if she did not stop her radical behavior. Sara would not. Sara became a mighty handmaiden for the Lord.

"Satan knew her potential, which is why he tried to destroy her early in life. Every chance she got she would warn her old girlfriends of the horrors of what they were delving into. Because of what she had seen, she warned all of the white witches about what they were doing, and she explained to all of them that they were deceived.

"They did not believe her and attempted kill her once by trying to place a spell on her and her family.

"You might think, how could school children be so vicious? But that is what Satan does. He perverts the innocent. She said her and her family was driving down the high way and for no reason at all, the car hit the edge of the concrete barrier and was thrusted at least 20 feet in the air.

"Sara said her entire family called on the name. It was then Sara said she felt the power of God grab the car and sit it down on the side of the road out of dangers way. It was just about that time that Father was traveling the opposite direction and said he noticed that he could see things moving in slow motion. So he knew the Lord was about to reveal something to him. It was at that hour that he saw their car hit the embankment and travel straight up in the air, he cried out to the Lord and he said he felt power go out of him and surround that car and sit it down easily. He then felt that same power, which felt bigger than the earth come quickly back inside of him.

"When he saw who it was, he stopped his car and assisted them. We found out about this because one of the wiccans told Sara what was done to her when she came to The Lords side. She explained, and that they had actually taken people's lives that way before but when Sara was saved, she knew her power was mightier than the power she had, so she renounced it and came to the Lords side.

"This whole story is in volume 37 I believe on the top shelf over there. She would then bring them to church one by one. She was an evangelist in her own right. Everyone would listen to Sara because she had done everything they were experimenting with.

"She had been one of the popular girls, but no longer cared about that. She just did not want to see any one go through the horror she had gone through. She would always say, 'Come to JESUS. It is the only way. Nothing else works.'

"Sara, Bud, Nina, Anna and I were the Holy Rollers of the school and we liked it. No one contended with us. We enjoyed our lives and wanted all of the other students to enjoy the freedom and the light we were living in as well."

Chapter 6

"Father waged war on the political front, after being elected to the school board. He knew how powerful the word of God was and fought to get the 10 commandments back in the schools. He tried to explain if you turn off the lights, the darkness automatically comes in. He made terrific grounds in that area.

"I became the chief Holy Rollers, as we were called, and started a Bible study in the school every morning. This was legal because it was student initiated and led. As long as it was student led, there was no breach of law.

"Many of the students began to come. We eventually took over the entire auditorium and had student led prayer. Our little group had done such a great job in exalting Jesus, that the media became aware of it. They had us on TV one day, under the title 'Students with a message.'

"I never forgot that. The night after we were on TV, I had a visit from my old father. He came to my home in the spirit, but could not get in, even though he tried desperately.

"The Lord woke me, and I could see him trying to get in our house in the spirit. I felt no fear, but spoke as I had been taught, 'In the mighty name of Jesus, leave this home and never return.'

"It looked as if he was snatched away quickly and never came back. I simply got back in the bed, and thanked God that I was protected, and slept like a baby.

"Mr. Ply had penetrated many homes that way. I had seen him do it. He would plant his ideas or take their lives. But blood bought Christians were protected. I could see he was very angry at the fact that he could not enter their homes. He had brought with him a mind control demon to attempt to destroy me. I could see it clearly. But God would not let it happen.

"My old father new where I was, and surely, he was upset that now I was on the other side. I was sure he would try again, but I know in whom I believe. I told father the next morning what had happened.

"He said, 'This is what happens to so called Christians all of the time. The dark side understands that, but the Christians not knowing what power they really have allow the darkness to come in and begin to oppress their children or them. Christians in this country are not aware of Satan's plans. We will win this battle for this community, district, region, and world in time.'

"Father would always declare.

"Bud, who was as big as any man, witnessed continually to the jocks, they listened to him because he was a one. He led the entire 8th grade football team to Christ. He became quite active in the Christian Athlete Organization. Winning souls by example. Bud had no shame, and use to say to me all of the time, 'We have got to write this stuff down and publish it one day, so the whole world will know the true power of God.' "I would reply what do you think the Bible is for" he would say "you know what I mean" and I did

"'I am praying for the Lord to raise up someone in my family to do just that.'

"I always agreed with Bud when he had powerful ideas like that, because I knew the Lord would honor it.

"Bud found out that there were a group of warlocks working in the school as well. These were the guys that got good grades and appeared to be great kids. Bud found out accidentally, when he was out late walking one Friday night.

"He said he just could not sleep so he asked his father if he could go for a walk just down to the school and back. When he got there, he went to the football field and saw several of the team chanting and sacrificing animals on the field.

"He recognized them all. They were dedicating their lives for victory in the upcoming football seasons. They dug up the field and placed amulets in it.

"'How foolish,' Bud thought. 'Your eternal souls for a football game?'

"When Bud got back home he told his father who prayed with him. Bud said he remembered falling right to sleep after that.

"During his study hall period, Bud went down to the football field and removed the amulets that had been placed there. Spoke the name and commanded whatever spirit that had come to the field to reveal itself. Bud said he did not know why he had said that but he did. He said he really did not expect anything to appear after all it was almost afternoon. But then he saw a shadow from what he thought might be a tree from the side, but it was not it was moving toward him with great speed.

"Bud said his first reaction was to run, but he remembered Pastor Anderson teaching, 'I have authority in this earth and I am taking this land back for God.'

"He spoke the name and as quickly as it started it stopped.

"'What is your name?'

"It said, 'False pride.'

"Bud spoke, and the angel that was standing on the school reached down, bound it, and cast it into a huge black whole that was over the field. Bud saw the angel in all of the Lord's glory, standing in battle mode. It then stood straight up after the demon was cast out and Bud said it seemed to disappear.

"The building had already been dedicated to God. Satan was attempting to take it back. The field felt clean after that. Bud knew that now he had to confront the players that had brought such a vile thing to the school.

"They just did not realize that even though they moved on, the spirits that they bring there stay there to contaminate other children until it is removed.

"After school Bud met with the quarterback to explain what had happened but he would not believe him and said prove it. Bud said no, but said he felt the Lord prompting him to do so.

"'If your God is greater than ours, than put my arms down.' It was known throughout the school that no one was as strong as Jessie Freemon, the varsity quarterback. Full grown men could not even get his arms down, when he stretched them out in front of him. He was that strong because of the spirits that worked in his life. Bud said fine and, with little or no effort, pushed his arms down to his side.

"'How is that possible? No one has ever been able to do that before!

"Bud said, 'It is simple. The power in me is greater than the power that is in you. I always marveled at witchcraft. Some thought you could be a good witch, but the truth is Satan is behind it all, he simply dresses it up different. Witchcraft is witchcraft. All of the power comes from Satan to deceive the children they had gotten everything they had ever wanted from witchcraft, by casting spells and incantation.'

"The team was number one in the community but it cost them their souls. Bud invited them all to the Church to see real power. And they all came.

"Nina met many witches and warlocks as well. They literally permeated the schools, because of the books they were required to read. They had all types of real spells in them and the children would experiment with them.

"Father was working very hard to have all of them removed, because they were as dangerous as how to make a bomb book would be.

"The children were bombarded with cartoons, tarot card games. Dabbling in the occult innocently, but becoming horribly hooked.

"Nina accidentally found out about another coven of witches. When she had, had a dream of one of Anna's friends casting a spell over the Bible study. Nina would always pray the night before a Bible study was to take place. The one time she did not, she could not open the doors for 15 minutes. It was then she remembered prayer. She did and the locks unlocked.

"The whole school was full of people delving in the occult. I thought, when do they have time to study? Bud had more incidents with the occult than any of us he would tell us all after the fact. Which is why he was always saying we have to write this down.

"He had met another young lady in the school who challenged him to see whose god was the strongest. But Bud would not compare our Lord to Satan. There was no comparison.

"'It was an insult,' he would always say, 'but I tell you what. If my God is the real God, it will start raining tomorrow at 5:00 a.m. and it will not end until 12:00 p.m.'

"We had had a drought that year, and was way below our rain levels. Bud had such faith in God he knew if he asked, his God would deliver.

"Sure enough, the next day it rained nonstop from 5:00 a.m. to 12:00 p.m.

"This was a perfect show of power for her, because her father was the local weatherman. She knew there was no rain in the forecast, and agreed.

"But Our God was able to do exceedingly, abundantly, above all that we can ask or think. She gave her life to Christ when she saw where the real power was, but she was tormented by the spirits that once possessed her and helped her.

"She invited Bud to her house when her parents where not at home, and they cleaned her room throughout all of her tarot cards, Ouija boards, dragons, crystal balls, everything. They put it all in a canister out in the back of the yard, but it would not burn.

"So Bud spoke the word of God and immediately the entire canister broke out in flames and the spirits that had possessed those items flew out into the air with a scream. Bud then went in and anointed the girl's whole home. The next week the girl and her entire family joined father's church.

"'How wonderful it is to have real power, and to know the true and living God,' Bud would always say.

He used to say to me, 'Since you will outlive me, promise me you will tell these stories to the whole world before you leave it.'

"I always promised I would, one way or another.

"Father continued the ministry Pastor Anderson had started and things had begun to change. The Ten Commandments, which had been taken out of the school, was now being put back under the History Banner of the school curriculum. Since this country was built on the Bible, why not?

"Father, who had been a lawyer, brought all of his legal skill to bear. He had gotten through the local courts, and now had it on appeal at the State Supreme Court. Father had mobilized all of the pastors in the community to pray and fast continually for this bill to pass.

"'The life of our children is in the balance.'

"So there was someone praying and fasting every single day of the trial. The warfare was violent. Mr. Ply was mobilizing his forces as well. He had organizations that were designed for that purpose alone.

"Keep the true God out of the schools, and they fought violently.

"But father's cry every morning, 'The kingdom of God suffereth violence and the violent take it by force,' (Matthew 11:12) and we as a family would always say Amen.

"The Professor who was retired helped father continually with his work. The Professor was a skilled communicator, and father would use him to speak on the radios and TV broadcast when they would cover these cases.

"Father's stand was always, 'God loves the children, and they should at least have the opportunity to know Him rather in school, the store, or a pubic park. After all we have him in our courts, on our money and in the American Constitution.'

"There was a constant barrage of intolerance of the Christian faith, toward people's lifestyles. The Professors favorite answer was, 'God loves them and so do I. However, I simply do not condone sin. It is destructive and will destroy a person, a community, a nation and, eventually, the world if allowed to run its course.'

"The founding fathers of America were being heralded as a bunch of slave owning hypocrites. The Professor who knew history of at least 100 cultures like the back of his hand simply said, 'They were men, just like you and I, with faults, just like you and I, but they, regardless of their human frailties, had a job to do for God, and that was to establish what would be the most powerful nation in the world. For those who owned slaves, they have had to stand before God. Let him be the judge. The Ten Commandments are a foundation. How about a school where there is no lying, stealing, murdering, or coveting? What person in their right mind would fight such a thing being taught to the children?'

"'Under the banner of separation of church and state.'

"'Poppycock,' he would say. 'You cannot remove God from anything. God still hears the silent prayer.'

"He would answer their insulting questions about the fact that yes, not all of the founding fathers were slave owners. And those that were, were wrong. But it still did not stop God from using them. So, should we throw the baby out with the bath water? The Professor always used very colorful language. The Ten Commandments are the foundation for every civilized community. Does that not exist in California? The founding fathers are dead and have had to stand before God themselves and be judged.

"But what they put together is magnificent, in every sense of the word, and cannot be disputed as the best way to govern people. One people, under God, indivisible, with Liberty and Justice for all.

"Every color, every race and both genders, male and female, needs to know that. Why push out what has worked for over 200 years in this country and your schools were at the top of the educational echelon, now there is so much disruption that they can barely be taught. You have children fighting children in your schools. You have, children disrespecting their teachers, boys dressing like girls and girls dressing like boys, and still, you fight to keep the one thing out of the schools that can help them. God allows men to choose, then God states to choose right.

"He would end every broadcast, regardless of radio, TV, paper, 'Who will you choose?'"

Chapter 7

"Father's stand was, 'Why not put it back in?'

"In Africa, Father had helped make the Bible a major textbook in the schools, and that alone brought peace to the community. Father had spoken to all of the other religious leader in the community. Muslim, Jewish, Catholic, and Hindu. All had no problem with the Ten Commandments. He got them all to sign a petition to have it put back in.

"'Who is fighting this,' Father would say to the media. "'Tell me who? What person in their right mind would attempt to keep light out of darkness, where our children are concerned?'

"But father and the Professor knew who it was. That was just for the media. They just kept the prayer vigil going. It never stopped. This went on for months. Then the night before the decision that was to be handed down, both father and I saw the war in the heaven in a dream.

"We both saw the state capital. It had a large steal chain wrapped around it. We both saw a sword come down from heaven and brake it. When I awoke, I ran to Father, who was always up before us, and said, 'Father! We won! We won! I saw it last night in my dream.'

"Father simply looked up from his word and said yes I believe you are right. We received a call before

Father left for work. The Ten Commandments are back. Father dropped to his knees and thanked God. He told the Professor on the phone, 'If my people who are called by my name would humble themselves and pray seek my face, turn from their wicked ways, then will I hear from heave and heal the land. Chronicalls 7:14. The healing is beginning.'

"As time went by Nina, Anna, Sara, and Bud and I would write down all of the times they saw the supernatural power of God work through them. I have over 200 books filled with the power of God being manifested, and Bud made me promise that I would put them in a book one day, and have them published for the whole world to see the true power of God in our day.

"Bud wanted his children to know. He said, 'The Lord had revealed to him that one of his children would write a book for the world to see and glorify God.'

"Bud seemed to always know I would out live him. I am not sure how, but he did and he made me promise that I would give these stories to someone in his family to publish.

"I always said I would, and Bud and the gang continually gave me stories of the supernatural power of God.

"My basement was totally full by the time I was through college. Bud would send them to me in the mail and always reminded me remember my promise. I would simply store them with the other books that

Sara, Anna, and Nina would send from college as well. Reading them simply made my faith grow, and caused me to grow in the Lord.

"Nina, Anna, Bud, Sara, and I became great friends. We had many adventures, the five of us. We all grew up in the same community. The one that stands out the most had to do with Sara. You remember the young lady that was in a mental institution? While Sara was in college, she had a friend that had gotten pregnant. Sara refused to tell her to go to the abortionist, which was legal at the time. She told her that regardless of how a baby comes to this Earth, God had a plan for them. Sara actually helped her conceal her pregnancy as long as she could, but about the seventh month it was becoming too difficult.

"She still was not sure how to handle it. She finally came to Father, who explained that she should have told her parents before now. So father brought the young lady and her parents into his office one evening, and Sara was allowed to attend and she told her parents about Michelle's baby, and that one day she knew he would be a mighty man of God. The parents were grieved but allowed Michelle to carry the baby and helped place it up for adoption. Sara attempted to keep track of the baby, and that child did indeed grow up. Sara never gave up on trying to keep tabs on the child, more so than Michelle. She eventually found out the child's name and monitored where he was and what he did his whole life.

"25 years later, it happened. One day while looking at the paper, Sara noticed a young man traveling overseas to preach the gospel. He was getting a lot of attention, because missionaries that had gone to that part of India did not return. It was then that she noticed right away that he looked just like Michelle, and felt the peace of God, knowing that God had spared his life to preach the Gospel throughout the world, just like God said he would. She called me to tell me about it, and we both rejoiced at God's wonderful plan for any human beings, regardless of how they got here."

"What was his name?"

"Only the most famous evangelist today. The Reverend John Davenport."

"The famous evangelist who preached in colosseums for 75 years. My parents still carry on about his crusades. He laid the ground work for much of their work. He started orphanages, hospitals in third world countries. He fed the hungry, opened schools and the list goes on."

Mr. Mike said, "Yes, the one and the same. As he laid the foundation for many ministries that are still in existence today, via colleges, hospitals and much more."

I remembered my history and how my grandparents would tell of his revivals on every Continent in the world. He has prayed with presidents. Eventually many of the abortion clinics became care centers for pregnant women for the entire nine months of pregnancy for the same amount of money it used to cost to kill the baby. Adoptions were also a part of the process, so if a woman did not want to keep her baby, it was legally adopted.

"Yes," Mr. Mike said. "Every child has a purpose, regardless of the circumstances surrounding how they got here.

"Bud went away to college on a football scholarship in New York City. Nina received an academic scholarship to the same university. Somehow, by the grace of God, we all managed to stay in contact with each other. Sara went away on a music scholarship in Virginia. Anna and I went to the community college right there in Perfect. I became assistant pastor of my Father's church.

"Upon completion of my Bachelor and Masters degree in Theology, Anna and I married. We had three children and took over the church, when my Father and Mother retired to Switzerland.

"Father had done great things for Perfect. Christian values were once again in the public schools. He had gotten several anti-God books out of the district, and had restored a respect for the church that had somehow gotten lost over the years. When he passed the baton to me, he said to me, 'You will strike the final blow, and Bud will hold it for the kingdom of God.'

"Father went back to Switzerland, and taught at a local Bible College until he retired there. He said he felt the Lord call him, to prepare the next generation for spiritual warfare. He passed away there, after living to the ripe old age of 100 years. Mother passed shortly after that. She was 98. I never forgot that Pastor Anderson had always said that that church would go to Bud one day. He said from the first day he laid eyes on that big dirty kid, he knew God had great things for him.

"When I left Perfect for another revival that had broken out in America, this time in Virginia, and was now sweeping the nation as a whole. I noticed that old principality my father and I had seen more than 15 years earlier.

"I had traveled many places, but this was only the second time I had seen the principality over America. As the plane began to ascend, I could see clearly the ruling principality.

"It was no longer powerful looking. It looked frail and weak. Its horns looked too heavy for its head. Its once massive throne looked like a small dining room chair. Its jewels were gone, and instead of thousands of demons reporting to it, I counted four.

"We had fought well, but knew the Christians in America would have to remain vigilant to get him totally off of that throne.

"I thought Bud would deliver the final blow when he returned from school." Mr. Mike continued, "Father and Mother called me to let me know that they had been fasting and praying for me. He said some demons can only be cast out with the combination of both. I went to the church that afternoon, when I returned from the revival, and I lay before the Lord, I opened my eyes and there it was. That principality of deception was standing in the sanctuary. It looked at me with intense hatred. It felt like knives cutting into my body. When I had seen it in the air, it looked weak, but now it looked huge and strong, and it had a large chain in its hand.

"It was then I saw the one I was named after. I finally got a chance to see Michael, standing there in all the glory of the Lord. He had a massive wingspan of about 15 feet width and length. They were pure white, trimmed in gold. He had on a breast plate of gold. His eyes were like fire and his face was like lightening. I watched as Michael lay hold of that principality, and take the chain it was holding and wrap it around it. He Shook the principality and what looked like gifts wrapped fell from it. Michael said, 'When the thief is caught, he must return all that he has taken, plus seven times more. The gifts that Satan has stolen from you he, has now returned sevenfold.'

"He smiled and vanished with the principality in chains and in hand.

"It was over. I had completed my task in America. After that, it seemed everything that I had been praying for began to come quickly to pass. State after state was being revived in the Lord. But the one thing I secretly prayed for more than just about anything else, was that my old father would be saved and that did look impossible. But I believed God.

"I did not know if the Lord would allow me to stay here long enough to see that, but I had hoped so. If not, I knew it would be left up to Bud to continue God's work in this great country, and I thought maybe it would take place on his watch.

"Mr. Ply became very ill, according to the newspapers, and was on his death bed. He would not allow them to put him in the hospital, but he stayed in his home wasting away from cancer of the brain.

"That is how Satan repays his servants. He helps them waste their lives with empty promises and leads them to a deplorable death, and then to the final place of torment…Hell. He had advanced cancer of the brain and he had been given less than three months to live. It was then I remembered what I heard my Father tell him not more than 10 years ago.

"God had let him live another ten years to make the right decision. The disease came on him suddenly while he was attending a very public political forum. They rushed him to the hospital and told him he was struck with cancer, and did not have long to live. He would not allow himself to remain in the hospital, so he was brought home. I knew he wanted to be home, so that he could conjure and attempt to heal himself as he did in the past. I had seen my old father heal others and himself of disfiguring diseases. Open tumors that I had seen literally fall off, and a man who was so disfigured that I could not tell he had a face until father conjured over him. I saw his face become whole.

"See, Satan does have power to heal but, requires a high price for it. Your soul.

"I knew this was the end for him because my real Father had already prophesied many years earlier that it would take place during this time. That night as I prayed, I fell asleep and found myself in Mr. Ply's home. I was in his room. He was surrounded by candles and beautiful lighted creatures that were soothing him telling him it was alright to come home now in Hell. The lighted spirits would escort him to his kingdom, not the scaly creatures he had control over, they were reserved for the darkside of Hell. Not where he would rule.

"I spoke to him and said, 'Do not believe them. They are lying to you, and they have been lying to you since the beginning.'

"They all turned on me and hissed. I commanded them to show him their true identity. Then suddenly they became dark, huge, green and scaly. They were fowl to the smell.

"I saw Mr. Ply sat up and said, 'OH NO! I was just about to leave the body for good, these were my guides to my throne in Hell. They were supposed to be pure to escort me to my eternal throne. What have I done?'

"I told him then and there, 'You have been deceived your entire life. Satan has totally deceived you, so you could do his bidding, and you have, you are now about to leave this earthly body permanently and you will lift your eyes up in a tormenting Hell, not a victorious Hell, if you do not accept Christ right now.'

"He dropped back to his bed, and the creatures around him began to back up as I came closer to him.

"I said, 'Father now you see the truth. This is your last chance. Who will you believe?'

"My old father exclaimed, 'But I have rejected Him my whole life. Why should He forgive me for all the harm I have caused Him?'

"'Simply because He loves you, and you were deceived as a young child. God has always known and is willing, even right now, to forgive, but you must make the decision for Christ now!'

"My old Father looked around the room at the creatures around the room that he had commanded for years, or so he thought, but now he saw their diabolical plot, which was to destroy his soul forever and ever.

"Then I said a silent prayer and remembered the words of Michael the archangel.

"'Satan has to return sevenfold what he has stolen because he has been caught.'

"The room itself began to shake. Satan himself was coming to collect this soul. Father had been possessed with thousands of demons and for decades had been Satans puppet.

"I was no match for Satan, but I remembered the scripture that said, 'Greater is He that is in me than He that is in the world.'

"When those words came out of my mouth, it was then I saw power like I had never seen before in my walk with God. I always thought God himself would have to contend with Satan but that was not the case. Satan is a created being, a fallen angel, and no match for Christ in me. He sent Michael once again, but this time he was much bigger and more powerful than before. Satan stood and drew a huge silver sword in chain, he looked massive.

"He had dark red skin, and eyes so black, it felt as if they were an abyss sucking you into evil when you looked at him. He had large black bat shaped wings, black finger nails like claws, huge black horns and bulging muscles.

"Michael, on the other hand, was bronze with wings that looked like eagles, pure white trimmed in gold. He has a massive golden sword, breastplate, helmet, sash shoes with shin guards, shield and a golden chain.

"Satan lunged to claim my old father's soul, but Michael stood between the two. As the swords collided, lightning sparked, which sounded like two tractor trailers crashing head on at full speed. It looked as if Satan was getting the best of Michael when I heard the Spirit of the Lord say, 'Pray.'

"So I began to. It was then when that I noticed that Michael began to overcome Satan. He grabbed him by his wings and wrapped them in the gold chain until he was bound. Once Satan was bound, what seemed like thousands of evil spirits that had possessed my old father were simultaneously bound with gold cords and vanquished right there in the room.

"Michael picked Satan up, and lunged him in what looked like an abyss that appeared in the room and then disappeared when he threw him in. Michael then turned and looked at me and disappeared as well.

"My old father who looked lifeless, sat up slightly, and said the sweetest words I had ever heard in my life. He said, 'Lord Jesus I am sorry. Please forgive me for all of my sins, and come into my heart. I accept you as Lord and Savior.'

"The moment he said that, more demons began to jump out of him. Hundreds. No, thousands of them! Screeching and screaming as if they were being tortured. They were now cast out and would have to report to the ruling principality that they had lost a regional warlock. Now their Hell would be severe, to say the least. I saw his face change from anger and hatred to calm and peaceful.

"He said to me, 'Please forgive me, my son, and thank you. Look over there. In my safe.'

"He gave me the combination. there is a list of every movie, every toy, every media idea that demons had been attached to enslave man kind in this region. He closed his eyes and he died.

"I went to the safe and took the papers. I then woke up with those papers in my hand. I read through them, and sure enough, all of the latest movies that were being shown were designed to put fear in people's hearts so that Satan could torment them.

"Elementary school children's toys, cards, and games had demons attached. Music, DVDs, certain videos that people were renting from video stores. Certain school aged books. Lawyers, judges, political officials, activists, and talk show hosts.

"All of these people and things had demons specifically assigned to them to do Satan's bidding. Some knowingly, for fame and power, and others unknowingly. Simply being used as puppets by doing what they thought was right, as opposed to doing what the Bible says is right. I turned the TV on that afternoon to see the report that Mr. Ply was found dead in his home. I was saddened for such a brilliant man, he had wasted his life for Satan. In the end, though, God had gotten all of the Glory.

"How merciful our God is, and though he does not tolerate sin, it does not matter what a man has done. JESUS died for us all.

"When Bud graduated with his Masters Degrees in Theology, he came back home and was voted as the new pastor of the church. He renamed it the Cornerstone upon his induction, and was determined that all that would happen within it would be done to please God. Pastor Darryl Alexander Thomas Mann".

"Mann, I exclaimed. "That is the man you were talking about. That is my last name."

"I know and you are the spitting image of your great, great, great, grandfather. You are the one I have been waiting for." He continued his story, "I turned all of Mr. Ply's paperwork over to Bud, and told him it was now his turn to watch, fight and pray for this region. He did just that. Churches all over America began to unite as one. Just like the very first church in the earth. I remembered as I left America I looked and saw only the Glory of God in the place where the principality of deception had reigned. It was gone. I had completed what God had for me to complete. Bud and Nina were married and had 4 boys.

"Those boys grew and pastored Cornerstone Church. And one of Bud's children have pastored ever since. I made him a promise when we were growing up. I told him that one day I would see that every adventure the five of us ever had would be published.

"The Lord had revealed to Bud that one of his children would publish our stories, and here you are. I have kept my word.

"It has been a pleasure meeting you. I always knew we would meet and it has been a pleasure. It's been a long wait but well worth it.

"All of these books belong to you. I had them professionally printed and bound for you, and I will have them shipped back to the states to your home address."

Mr. Mike stood up, and gave me a great big bear hug. He said, "I will tell your great, great, great, grandfather that you have grown into a fine man, and that I have kept my word."

He then got up and said good night.

I stood there dumbfounded.

The oldest man in the world was a distant relative of mine.

I picked up all of my things. It was about 9:00 pm, and I went back to town, still speechless.

When Zahede picked me up, he asked what was wrong, but I just couldn't articulate it.

It was too much for any mind to comprehend. We drove silently back to the city. Zahede helped me get my things to my room and said good night.

I apologized for my silence and asked him to pick me up tomorrow morning at seven so that I can go out and say my final goodbyes to my great, great, great granduncle.

He looked puzzled, and simply said, "See you in the morning."

I slowly pealed my clothes, and collapsed into the bed. I don't recall even falling asleep that night. It was morning as soon as my head hit the pillow.

The next morning, when Zahede picked me up, he told me, "You were the one that Mr. Mike had been talking about. He always said that a relative was destined to tell the story. Whereas I had my suspicions about you being related to him, when I found out you were writing his story, my paper did a genealogy tree on you and found out where you were from. Once we found out you were from the same place Mr. Mike had done great exploits for the Lord, we knew."

He smiled warmly and said, "Congratulations! What a wonderful family of warriors you belong to."

The time seemed to fly. I would normally notice all of the beauty around me, but I was so caught up in what God had done in my own life, that I was very reserved in my speech. I stepped out of the jeep and opened the little white picket fence and walked through the field of small pastel butterflies, to the immaculately kept home.

Mr. Mike met me at the door and said, "Come. Walk with me. I am sure you have many questions."

We walked through the house, out of the back door, and down the stairs on a path that he had carved out over the years of walking through the jungle.

"Aren't you afraid of all of the wild animals in the jungle?"

"No," he smiled. "I don't bother them, and they don't bother me."

It was then that I saw a whole pack of lions, at least 10 feet away. It was if they did not see us.

Mr. Mike continued to speak, but I was focused on the lions who did not blink an eye when we walked literally right in front of them. He smiled and said, "That is Leo's clan."

"You know the wild animals by name?"

"Yes, I do. We speak every morning," he said laughingly. "So what would you like to know?"

I asked, "Why was this kept from me? Surely my father new the prophesy."

"Yes, he did, but he did not have to reveal it to you. He knew God would. The desire was put in you to write, while you were still in the womb. You have become what you were created to become. The prayer of the family was that God would get the glory from the books that you would publish. When you were born with this burning desire to be a journalist, everyone knew. Surely, you recall a few stories being told about the Journalist to come?"

"Well yes I remembered, but I never thought it would be me, I thought it would be hundreds of years past my time. I always thought father was a little disappointed I did not want to become a minister. He never really acknowledged my talent in this area."

Mr. Mike said, "Are you sure? Did you not get a full ride journalistic scholarship to a university in America?"

"Well yes."

"How do you think you got in?"

"I never did know that. I just did. I never really applied for a scholarship."

"No, but your father did. He was always in your corner."

"Mr. Mike you are 115 years old. There is something I have been wanting to find out, since we met two weeks ago."

"What," Mr. Mike asked.

"How do you remain in such good shape?" I asked this, because I was having trouble keeping up with him as well.

"I'd like to say I just live right and eat well, and I do those things. In all honesty, though, it is appointed to every man to be born, and to every man to die, and my time was not complete, until I was able to share these stories with the world, so that they would know that every man, woman, boy, and girl on the face of this planet is in a warfare. Whether they acknowledge God or not. They must choose.

"There is only one enemy. Satan. He simply works through people, tell them in every book you publish if they do not chose JESUST CHRIST," he said, very reverently, "that they have chosen Satan by default. No choice is a choice for Satan.

"You see, Satan desires to deceive human beings, and he does, which is why you have a lot of sincere people, but on the wrong side."

"But I know a lot of wonderful people in other religions."

"As do I," he said, "and I pray for them as they pray for me. However, I pray every day and every night so that the true light will be revealed to them, before they leave this Earth. Remember the acronym BIBLE. Basic Instructions Before Leaving Earth.

"Yes. Father quoted it probably every day of my life."

"Love all men and show them the love of Christ. True Christians live in love. Not hate. That is a lie that the world believes about the church. Teach them all how much God really loves all mankind, and it does not matter who they are or what they have done. The Lord died for them all. The whole world.

"My old father, Mr. Ply, was a wicked man, serving Satan, until right before he died, but God showed mercy on him. God's desires for all mankind to live with Him, for all eternity, in Heaven. He truly loves us.

"Show them in the BIBLE. That an almighty GOD sent his son for the salvation of all men. It is only Satan who comes to steal, kill and destroy. Always remember that."

I asked one last question. "Why does the name of Jesus mean so much to you?"

Mr. Mike stopped walking, placed both hands over his chest and his eyes welled up with tears as his lower lip trembled, and he said in a hush tone, "He saved my soul from eternal separation from Him, He loved me when no one els did. JESUS. It is the name that is above every name. Though Satan attempts to make it common by causing people to use it in a curse word. It still stands alone as the only name by which all men must be saved. Convey this to the people. JESUS CHRIST is LORD, and he died for all mankind, rather they accept him or not.

"Have you noticed no won has a problem in acknowledging who Satan is but everyone is confused on how to get to GOD? Tell them to try the Lord. That is Satan's job, to keep man confused. Just tell them to call him JESUS," he said with great vigor. "He will answer, and against him, Satan is no match. You will hear statements like that is too much. You can't believe such stories. I respond by asking why is it you can have too much God but not too much cursing, drinking, vulgarity, deviant behavior, violence and the list goes on? All these things are designed to destroy man, but God. God loves man. So much so, that he sent JESUS. Convey that in all of your books, and the Lord himself will do the rest."

It was at that point I found us back at the home. As we walked in, I could smell breakfast. Mrs. Dottie came out and said, "Would you like to stay for breakfast?"

"No. I have to catch a plane. It leaves at eleven this morning. But thank you, it has been a pleasure."

She smiled and said, "Likewise."

"Don't forget to send me the book as soon as it is published. I will be leaving soon."

"Oh? Where are your going?"

He smiled gently and gave me a bear hug, and said, "Heaven son. Heaven."

I turned and walked away, knowing that I would never see him again on this Earth but by the time I reached Zahede's jeep, I knew I would see him in Heaven one day. We took off, back to the city, stopped off at the hotel to pick up my things and checked out.

The manager smiled and said, "I look so forward to reading your book."

"Thank you," I said, smiled, and walked away.

Zahede took me to the airport, and shook my hand fervently. "I look forward to reading your book. It has been an honor meeting you."

I took my things and boarded my plane, wondering if it was possible for me to see into the spirit?

I never had before.

I looked toward the heavens as we began to ascend and saw nothing but blue sky and white fluffy clouds. I lay back and play the story that Mr. Mike had told me from start to finish, I barely got through with a fourth, and I was at home. I had more than 100 hours' worth of tape.

What a wonderful book this would be. I deplaned at about 9:00 a.m., Washington time.

I found my car, and went straight to the office. When I arrived, my very anxious editor asked so how was it.

"Absolutely astounding," I said.

"Get right to the editors with your information," he said. "Did you get plenty of pictures?"

"Yes I did. But you will not believe how this 115-year-old man looks."

He smiled and said, "I don't care. I want this story out in tomorrow's newspaper. So hop to it!"

I grabbed my equipment, and went to editing. I had so much information, my cultural story literally took up a whole page in the paper. This was unheard of for this type of story, but because reporters had been trying to get this man's story for decades, it was allowed.

The *Post* had it. What an honor.

When I arrived home, I called my father again and said, "Dad, why did you not tell me that Mr. Mike was a relative?"

He said, "He was a distant relative but we all knew your destiny was to publish his life story. My father passed the truth to me, and his father before him, and his father before him. Your mother and I knew from your earliest years that you were the one to fulfill such a mission.

"You have been writing since you were a toddler Your life was consumed with being a journalist. We just waited for God to work his plan in you, and he did."

I did publish my book and I called it *Michael (A Holy Ghost Story)*. The book literally transformed lives and sold millions around the world.

I sent the very first copy to Mr. Mike, who called and thanked me.

I attempted to call him to let him know that I had started on combining several of the stories that he had sent me for publishing as well. But when I called, Mrs. Dottie answered the phone, to tell me that Mr. Mike had went home to be with the Lord.

She said, "When he had gotten everything in order, and when he got your book, he went into his study and read it. He called me in to let me know that you had done an excellent job. He wanted to tell you, but could not reach you by phone, so he left you a voice message."

"Yes, I got it."

"He went to bed that night, and just didn't wake up the next morning. The doctor said he died of nothing. He just went to sleep."

I smiled to myself, knowing that I was a part of such a glorious life.

"By the way, he also left you the dinette set. He said he thought your new wife might like it."

I said, "You know I am not married."

I knew that, but that was probably about to change.

I hung up the phone and felt strangely fulfilled. As if I finally knew what I was to do in the Earth. Tell all mankind that there is a battle waging for the souls of men, and that Satan is no match for the true in living God through JESUS CHRIST.

But man must choose.

Michael. What a perfect name for a true warrior of God.

There is a war going on, I thought and the question I put at the end of every book, including this one, is simply, **"Whose side are you on?"**